TERROR FROM THE DEEP

ALEX LAYBOURNE

SEVERED PRESS
Hobart Tasmania

TERROR FROM THE DEEP

WWW.SEVEREDPRESS.COM

This novel is a work of fiction. Names, characters, places and incidents
are the product of the author's imagination, or are used fictitiously.
Any resemblance to actual events, locales or persons,
living or dead, is purely coincidental.

ISBN: 978-1-925493-89-4

CHAPTER 1

The fist did not break his nose, but caused sufficient damage to produce a thick stream of warm blood. From his position on the floor, Troy Deane could do nothing but shake his head, trying to clear his jarred brain and spur him back to life.

The man on top of him would not stop until he knocked Troy out, or until the referee called a stop to the match. Both options were a direct contradiction to Troy's own plans.

Troy felt his opponent adjust his position, as he tried to move past his guard and into the full-mount. Experience told Troy he only had one shot, so he waited, lowering his leg just a little, helping his opponent to move towards the mount. With a wild thrust, Troy drove his hips upward, and twisted his upper body.

With his opponent caught momentarily off guard, Troy spun and slid out through the man's legs. It was a risky move, but the only option Troy had, if he wanted to continue fighting, and stop being used as a punch bag. For a heart-stopping moment, Troy left his body fully exposed, giving up his back in order to escape. If his opponent reacted quickly enough, or predicted his escape attempt, then he would be helpless to a submission move.

Troy scrambled backward, freed himself, and jumped to his feet. The crowd went wild, cheering and hollering their appreciation. Troy pushed the din to the back of his mind. His years competing in the cage taught him that all the majority of the crowd only wanted to see flying fists and feet, and blood, they always wanted blood. Many found the technical aspect of fighting and grappling too boring and slow. They wanted action, and lots of it.

Troy felt the cage against his back, and took a step away. He needed room to work. Mark Hunter turned and moved to engage.

With no time to breathe, they came together again. Hunter was a remarkable fighter, and at twenty-four years of age, many regarded him as being the brightest prospect in the game. A naturally light-footed light heavyweight, he moved like a man several weight classes lower, but packed a heavyweight's punch. Quick and solid in wrestling, he represented the complete MMA package.

Shooting for a takedown, Hunter came in low. He telegraphed the move; one of his favourites. When he smelled blood, Hunter became as predictable as an amateur. He would look to take the fight to the floor and work the ground-and-pound.

Troy moved ever so slightly and caught the man as he ran through. His arm slid around Hunter's chest. He moved to grab his left arm with his right, but Hunter's power carried them both through too far. For a moment, Troy found himself fully inverted as he spun over Hunter's back. Landing on his feet, the rest of his body followed through. Hunter left the floor, twisted in a way that left him defenseless.

Troy gave a roar as he threw his opponent over his hip and onto the floor. Hunter's head bounced on the hard canvas base, and brought the crowd to their feet.

The upkick flashed toward him. Troy weaved out of the way with ease and dropped his body forward, his large fist swinging towards his opponent's unguarded chin. The moment the shot landed, the balance of the bout shifted.

His fist caught Hunter on the jaw, and for a moment, his hands dropped away, leaving Troy free to swing with his fists, landing land three clean shots, bloodying up his opponent's face.

The bell rang, and for a moment, Troy thought the ref had stopped the match.

"You got this in the bag," Troy's trainer spoke as he fell onto his stool. His nose burned from the shot he had taken, but the flow of blood could be stemmed, and his vision had returned to normal. "You've got one more round, and he's going to fall. You hurt him at the end. You hurt him bad. Keep working your boxing. Low kicks to the outside; he's favoring his left leg. I want to see a low kick followed by hard combinations. Punches in bunches, baby, punches in bunches."

Troy sat on his stool, and listened to the instructions Freddie Barone gave him. He nodded and allowed the strategy to form in his mind. He flinched as Terry, his cut man, worked on his nose, and drank when Joe pushed the water bottle into his mouth. Yet for the whole minute he sat on the stool, he never took his eyes off the opposite corner.

At thirty-six years old, many thought Troy's best days were behind him, but he had fought his way back to the top, taking out the younger man in one grueling match after another. He had fought more times than could possibly be considered healthy. If not for a two-year break as the result of a career-threatening knee injury, he would have been a champion many years ago and most likely retired by now. Through the years, Troy had learned one key thing about the break in between rounds. What the coach had to say was important. His instructions were to be trusted and followed, allowing a little room for individual creativity. The key thing to do was to watch the opposition corner. Troy could tell a lot about how a fight was going based on what happened during the round break. If the corner was frantic, rubbing and wiping in their attempts to stop the bleeding, then he knew he had the guy on the ropes.

More often than not, he would hold his gaze long enough to make eye contact with his opponent. In those moments, just before the round started and the fighters got back to their feet, that the game faces slipped and the real faces could be seen.

"You got this. Knock this guy out and we are the number one contenders. This is your time, baby. Your fucking time." Freddie and Troy went way back. They started working together long before the big time promotions came calling. Their relationship went beyond that of coach and student, it went deeper than father and son. They were brothers in arms, bonded and forged in the blood of the battlefield.

The bell rang and the two warriors moved into the middle of the cage. Troy studied his opponent, his eyes locked on his face. There, the moment, the look. He strode forward, his chest puffed out, his aching back straight. He could taste victory. They touched gloves and the final five minutes began.

Hunter feinted for a takedown, hoping to trick Troy into a reaction. Troy stood firm and threw a stiff jab. He followed this with a quick combination. He pushed forward, throwing bombs, backing his opponent up. He ducked and dodged a head kick, but found himself turned around. In an instant, Hunter assumed control and pinned him against the fence. The cold wire of the cage pressed into his back, his opponent pressing into him from the front. Hunter drove his shoulders against Troy's chest.

Troy couldn't breathe. He gasped for breath, punching and pushing trying to find a way to free himself. He threw out his knee, connecting with something. He adjusted his grip on his opponent's shoulders and threw another knee. Hunter buckled from the blow. Another knee and he could shove himself free. Hunter moved back, while Troy pushed himself from the cage. He threw a kick, aiming for the welt that had risen on Hunter's thigh.

He dropped his left shoulder but came through with a right hook. His fist caught Hunter on the chin and sent him stumbling. He wheeled his arms as he moved backwards, stunned. Troy ran, leaping into the air, cocking his right hand as he rose, and throwing it forward as he came down. The Superman Punch was a weapon Troy loved to use in a fight. He caught Hunter flush and sent the man to the canvas. Troy landed hard and froze for a moment as pain tore through his right knee. Fueled by adrenaline, however, Troy lunged at his downed opponent, throwing a succession of hammer fists to the side of Hunter's bloodied face.

The crowd went wild, driven on by the sight of blood and the looming upset victory. Troy was lost to the moment, the pain in his knee forgotten. He didn't hear the ref calling for the bell, and got in one more hammer fist before the big man in the striped shirt threw himself between the pair.

The fight was over. Troy had won. He fell to the floor, hands covering his face as he raised his head to the heavens. His redemption had arrived.

Troy's corner crew mobbed him, while the medical staff busied themselves with Hunter, who was still lying on the floor. Troy waited, not wanting to celebrate just yet. His opening came, and he moved forward to check on his opponent's condition. His leaping blow broke Hunter's jaw, the resultant hammer fists causing all manner of trauma to the nose and mouth area.

Troy refused to celebrate his win until the doctors had told him Hunter was alright. He embraced the man who had pushed him to the limit, and then turned to his corner, ready to party.

Long after the crowd had started to make their way home, Troy still sat in the changing rooms. He was naked, not even wearing a towel to cover his modesty. He had a bag of ice strapped to his knee. He did not hear Freddie come in, or acknowledge his presence until his trainer clapped him on the shoulder.

"You did it, kiddo. I knew you had it in you." Freddie looked to be just as happy as Troy at the victory. Not surprising, as technically Freddie retired three years earlier when he turned sixty-two, but he kept Troy on the books, and now he too found rejuvenation in his boy's second wind.

"Yeah, but my knee popped out when I hit that superman. Damn thing just went as I landed." Troy winced as he tried to stretch his injured leg.

"Well, we ain't spring chickens anymore. Aches and pains is just part of growing old. The title fight won't be for a while yet, so we have plenty of time to piece you back together, Humpty Dumpty." Freddie slapped his hand on Troy's bare back and leaned in close, so their heads were touching. "I love ya, kiddo."

"Thanks. I think I need a holiday. A little bit of fun in the sun." Troy raised his head, his movements slow and sluggish. Everything ached, and in the morning, it would only be worse.

"I don't blame you. I tell you what, they just opened this new place down in Mexico, a resort of something. My daughter was just talking about it the other day. It's some super special island they built or something. You like the water, they got all sorts of diving, and snorkeling shit going on." Freddie stood in the middle of the locker room. "Take a break, champ. We will be waiting when you come home." Freddie turned and left, leaving Troy to his thoughts.

He always took his time after a fight. There was a process involved. The fight game was not a pretty one. The man he became inside the cage was a different beast to the man who lived outside of it. Everybody talked about prepping for a fight, about getting into the zone. What they didn't mention was getting back out again once the fight ended. Troy needed the time after the fight to reflect, to allow his body to calm, transition back into the outside the ring persona.

A single man, with no ex-wives or children he could go and visit, Troy led a simple life. He had amassed enough money to keep himself going after retirement, but not enough to live a life of leisure.

Leaving the stadium, he drove home to his apartment. A nice building with good tenants, the living areas were spacious enough to meet Troy's minimal needs and tastes. He stopped at a hamburger restaurant on the way home. The visit was one of the older components of his post-fight ritual. So much so that after several years of the same process, the manager was always conveniently placed behind the drive through window just as Troy came in.

Troy's knee ached by the time he closed his apartment door and placed his greasy dinner on the table. By the time he went to bed, the joint became stiff and tender to the touch. Come morning, the swelling had set in, the joint growing to twice its normal size.

Troy did not have to try hard to find the place Freddie had mentioned. The website painted the resort to be a haven, a safe place of refuge for those looking for a stylish getaway. Fully inclusive, it had everything Troy wanted in a holiday. The holiday would be Troy's first real break from life since his accident. He had been training every day, trying to claw his way back up the rankings.

He booked the ten-day break before lunch, and spent the afternoon packing. He didn't leave for two days, but wanted to gauge how much he still needed to buy in order to be ready.

Troy tried his best to ignore his knee, but by the time midday rolled around, the swelling had not gone down, and the pain refused to budge. Limping through his flat, Troy pulled out a lock box and twisted the rollers to the correct combination. He sat down at his dining table, pulling out a syringe and a small vial of fluid.

Troy winced as he jabbed the needle into his swollen joint. The cortisone did not stand any chance of curing his knee, but the jab would buy him some time, and at least let him get to Mexico. Once there, he would rest it, maybe even get a massage or two.

Everybody left Troy alone for the first day after his fight. Another custom that had built up over the years.

Troy understood the concern in Freddie's voice when he called him early that afternoon.

"Everything okay?" his coach asked.

"Yep, all good at this end. I just wanted to let you know I've booked a break at that place you mentioned. I have to say, the place looks good." Troy sat on his sofa, his leg resting on the coffee table, further elevated by a pile of cushions.

"That's great, kiddo. You need a rest. When do you leave?"

"Tomorrow."

"Perfect. How's your knee?"

"Still there. I just needed to get some sleep," Troy lied. "You were right, it's just age playing tricks on me."

"I'm glad. Where's your head at?" Freddie made no attempt to hide his concerns.

"I'm tired, and sore, but I'm the number one contender, baby. I'm ready for Hendricks," Troy lied.

"That's my boy! Well, you take your rest, kiddo, and when you're back, we're going after the gold."

CHAPTER 2

Deep beneath the ocean surface, a shark swam. The light did not penetrate so far into the water, but the shark did not need to see in order to hunt. It could sense the presence of prey all around it. The sea was full of nourishment. Its kingdom had no boundaries.

The shark moved through the water; its senses were on fire, impulses came from everywhere. They moved in a wave, hitting the beast from all sides. They were enough to disorient the creature and leave it close to stationary, something the shark could ill-afford.

The rumble rolled through the water, and while the shark could not see it, the seabed shook. A small crack traced along the ground, running in a jagged line along the edge of the quake. The gap widened as the pressure from beneath the earth's crust found a release. The rush of bubbles hit the shark, startling the creature.

The shark was big. It knew this. While not the largest thing in the ocean, the shark was larger than most. It did not know fear, even when up against bigger creatures. Yet as the rumble subsided, and the rush of bubbles reduced, something had changed in the water.

The change was subtle; other creatures in the area did not seem to notice. The school of fish that passed above the shark seemed oblivious. The shark was a greater predator than them, able to sense such changes to the environment, and able to understand that it was in a bad place.

The shark turned around, swimming out into deeper waters. The cracks in the ocean floor deepened, widening until the shark could sense the movement coming from beneath.

Hunger kicked in. A need to feed, regardless of whether what it sensed was a source of sustenance or not. The shark angled its body and sank deeper, its belly scratching on the seabed.

The strong impulses came in a rush. The shark pushed its body forward at a faster pace, racing through the water, diving, its mouth poised to snatch anything that came its way.

Powerful jaws opened; long, thick teeth were barred in the darkness. The shark dove, its hunger growing like a rage. Jaws snapped shut, the body thrusting itself forward. The shark felt pain, and then nothing. The fight was over, and two of the three sections of its body fell away from the giant mouth and floated down to the seabed. Blood further clouded the disturbed water, shrouding the giant beast as it pushed its body through the crack in the ground.

The taste of blood and flesh filled its head with sensations long since forgotten. The beast had risen, and the world regained its top predator.

The two remaining sections of the great white hit the seabed and were instantly attacked by the beast's offspring. Their hunger equal to their mothers, their existence driven by the need to kill and feed. Hunger was all they understood. The remains of the shark were destroyed, even the bones crushed and remaining fragments pulled away by the tide.

The sea settled, the change to their ecosystem not yet recognized, but the creatures were hungry, and could sense where the best food lay. They moved in a group, a gang intent on destroying anything that crossed their path.

CHAPTER 3

Sonia Marcos was sitting in the kitchen area of the *Amity Three* research vessel two miles off the Mexican coast. She couldn't sleep, a strange occurrence for her, especially when out on the water. Normally, the rocking of the boat and the peace she found on the ocean lulled her to sleep in a matter of moments.

Something troubled her, played with her mind and made her restless, but she could not put her finger on what exactly. Their trip was almost over, and so far, they had found nothing in the water to cause alarm. The traces of the rig accident several months earlier were all but gone. After an extensive clean-up operation, the ocean took over and started to heal itself.

Even the calm weather and flat seas did little to soothe the uneasy feeling churned in Sonia's gut like bad sushi.

Pushing the glass of water away, Sonia rose and walked through the ship up to the deck. She tried to be as quiet as possible. The steps creaked, regardless of how much pressure was applied to them, but she reached the deck without causing any undue commotion.

The night air was warm, stiflingly so. If Sonia had not checked the weather reports seven times that day, she would have put money on a storm rolling through come daybreak. Sonia turned her eyes to stars, their multitude creating just enough light to keep the simmering beauty of the ocean visible. The full moon was also a sight to behold, especially out on the water, away from the hustle and bustle of urban life.

Sonia leaned over the edge of the boat, resting her arms on the railing, letting her hands dangle over the edge.

She stared at the water, her mind drifting away as the hypnotic power of the ocean dragged her into the happy place she so often went to.

When it came, the rumble hardly registered on the surface. Not the first wave at least. Sonia felt it, but only because she stood in a state close to a trance. The second rumble carried like a whisper from a dream. The water rippled a little. The boat vibrated as if a shiver passed through it.

Sonia turned, her skin caressed with goosebumps. Nothing changed. The night sky remained clear and the rest of the five-man crew slept soundly below deck. They were crammed into quarters designed for three, and even then comfort seemed lacking.

Under most circumstances, the *Amity Three* operated with a crew through the night, either moving to a new location or taking advantage of the quiet to document findings and carry out the more time-consuming tests and investigations.

This smooth nature of the current trip put them all at ease, however, and the need for shifts fell away, meaning everybody got to catch up on some sleep. A close-knit group, nobody minded the extra bodies in the sleeping quarters. Nobody other than Andrew, but he was a special case. He fell on the autism spectrum, and while his work and interactions were rarely affected, when it came to sleeping, he needed his space. The crew understood this, and made the necessary exceptions as a result. He belonged to their family. They had been working together a long time, across many countries.

The third rumble was harder, more discernable than the previous two. The physical disturbance on the ocean surface caught Sonia's attention. She moved to lean over the railings. Underwater quakes were not uncommon, but her gut told her something was amiss; something more than a quake. Something was not right. Around the boat, the water rippled. Something moved, breaking the surface with an angry thrash.

Sonia jumped as something impacted against the hull. It was a dull, meaty thwack, hard enough to rock the boat. A second and a third thud soon followed. Sonia's first thought told her something was pelting the bottom of the boat, possibly a dolphin or some other larger animal trapped beneath the boat, their mind set on going through rather than around.

"What's going on?" the sleepy voice of Clark Wilson spoke out.

"No idea, I think we had a quake," Sonia answered, turning toward the figure as he emerged onto the deck. Wearing nothing but a white T-shirt and a pair of boxers, his long greying hair a wild bushel around his head, he cut quite the mad scientist figure.

"Do we have the monitors running overnight?" he asked, suddenly awake.

"I think so, we should ask Barry, but let's not wake them."

"What time is it anyway?" Clark asked.

"You know, you really should just start wearing a watch," Sonia said.

"Nope."

"A cell phone at least."

"Never. When I work I work, so I am here. When I don't I am at home, so people can call or visit me. Email is bad enough," Clark answered, scratching his head.

"You are a character, Clark. Well, it is a little before three, so let's leave them to sleep," Sonia answered.

"Sounds like a fair plan. But quake or not, what the heck keeps crashing against the hull? That was what woke me."

"I have no idea, probably a school of Mahi or something. Quake could have spooked them, driven them to the surface," Sonia replied.

"Maybe."

At that moment, something struck the hull again. Something larger than before, for the boat rocked heavily back and forth. The water around them churned and frothed.

"There you have them," Sonia said as she and Clark moved to the side of the boat.

"They don't look like Mahi," Clark said leaning over the side. "Quick, grab me a light."

Sonia turned to grab one of the handheld spot lamps. She grabbed the closest one and turned, just as a large splash caused water to slap against the side of the boat and onto the deck.

"Woah, they are wild," Sonia said as he turned. Her words dissolved into a scream as Clark turned to face her.

The fish was at least three feet long, and while the body started thick at the head, the torso tapered down to a narrow point before its tail fin sprouted. The body thrashed from side to side, spraying blood in all directions. Clark's cries for help were muffled by the creature eating his face.

As the body thrashed in the dark, blue lights seemed to spark along its flank.

Sonia's screams brought others running out onto the deck. They came to a sudden stop the second they took in the sight of their colleague struggling against the giant fish.

Clark held the flapping fish in both hands, but the muscular body contracted and contorted, too powerful for anybody to hold.

The fish came away on its own accord a few moments later, pulling Clark's face with it. The fish fell to the deck, landing in a puddle of blood. Thrashing with its powerful body, the creature inched its way to the edge of the deck. Squirming beneath the side, it disappeared back into the ocean, landing with a heavy splash.

Clark remained standing, blood gushing from the raw meat pulp that was his face. One eyeball lay on the flood, the other hung level with the holes of his nose, bouncing on the optic nerve like a child's toy. The nose itself was gone, chewed through by the razor sharp teeth that had filled the fish's mouth to the point of overflowing.

Cheeks, lips, flesh, meat, cartilage and bone, all of it missing, stripped away by the creature in a single, effortless attack, leaving Clark looking like a man abandoned mid-way through a face lift.

Everything seemed to come to a stop. Clark remained standing for what seemed like an age, when in truth it lasted no more than a few seconds. Clark let out a gargled groan, and blood bubbled from the dark hole that was his mouth. He fell to the deck, still. His face made a wet, meaty slap as it hit the wooden surface.

Sonia stepped back, numb. With the frenzy of the attack, and the screams of those around her, she hoped that, whatever it was, the worst was over; that the creatures would leave the boat alone.

The *Amity Three* lurched in the water as something buffeted them from below. The hull jumped from the water, sending the four remaining crewmembers flying, while Clark's corpse slid through the bloody puddle like a gore-dribbling snail.

"What was that?" Nadia cried out. She lay on the deck with a trickle of blood running down her face.

"I don't know. There was a quake and, those things just went nuts," Sonia said, regaining her feet. She had fallen against the wall, her leg colliding with one of the many housings, fitted to hold their equipment while working. As a result, she could no longer feel anything more than a dull pulse from her hip all the way down to her feet.

"Did you see that thing?" Ian asked.

"I've never seen anything like it," Nadia replied.

"It looked like a viperfish," Ian added.

"I've never seen a viper that big before, have you? That thing had to have been close to five feet long," Nadia answered.

"I know, but I'm just saying, that is what it looked like," Ian fired back, snapping.

"We are taking on water." Barry ran back onto the deck. Nobody had seen him disappear.

"What?" Sonia asked,

"Whatever hit us, managed to tear a hole in the hull. We are taking on water," Barry wheezed. The damage done by years of chain-smoking were still evident, even though he had finally quit the habit the year before.

"Can we pump it away?" Nadia asked.

"I don't think so," Barry replied.

"We are two miles from shore, we can take the dinghy," Ian offered, his initial snappy mood gone in the face of crisis.

"I don't think those things will let us get very far," Sonia said.

As if to prove her point, the boat lurched heavily. The attack came from the port side, pushing the boat over towards the ocean. Barry cried out as he slipped in a puddle of Clark's blood and toppled over the railing.

Fish jumped at him as he fell. By the time his body hit the water, his guts had already spilled from the hole their mouths had torn. The frothing water turned pink when the corpse splashed down.

The boat continued to lurch, leaning further and further until water washed over the deck.

The others hung on as fish leaped towards them. One collided head first with the iron wall behind Sonia. The heavy impact was hard enough to dent the surface, but also enough to crack the fish's head and shower Sonia with its blood.

The boat fell back down flat, leaving Sonia, Nadia, and Ian huddled together on the deck. They sank fast, the water lighting up around them, as if electrified. The blue flashes came and went as the first rose to the surface to crash against the boat, only to sink back down below.

"We cannot just stand around here waiting," Sonia screamed, limping over towards the life raft. The small boat hung on the port side of the craft.

"Those things will kill us the minute we hit the water," Ian called after her.

"We are dead anyway," Sonia replied.

She reached the craft and began to work on loosening the restraints that held the emergency dinghy in place. With one half done, the craft swung inwards, meaning Sonia had to lean over the railings to reach the second connector.

"Give me a hand," she called out, hoping that either Ian or Nadia was standing behind her.

Water splashed against her face, and a pain cut into her side. Sonia opened her eyes. A three-foot-long fish hung from her flank, its teeth hooking through her ribcage, tearing flesh and snapping bone as the powerful jaws closed.

She tried to scream, but couldn't. A second fish launched itself and tore her throat out in a shower of warm blood and gristle. The water churned as the taste of her blood excited the predators beneath her. A large mouth, with teeth easily six inches long, came up from the water. The jaw opened and closed around Sonia's slender frame. The creature tore her body in two, and sank back beneath the surface with a mouth full of flesh and a craving for more.

Nadia screamed, frozen in mid-reach. Sonia's remaining upper half still held onto the remaining life raft connector, a single shoulder, head, and partial torso. The weight of her frame unclasped the boat and both the dinghy and what remained of Sonia tumbled into the water. Within moments, the wood splintered and the craft was dragged down into the ocean.

Water flooded over the bow, charging towards them.

"What do we do?" Nadia cried.

Ian looked at her, knee deep in water. He opened his mouth to speak, but a large viperfish leaped from the water and took his head off with a single snap of its jaws. Blood spurted from the bloody neck stump like a fountain.

Nadia was alone. Something brushed against her leg. She jumped and spun around, catching a glimpse of the blue lights shimmering on the fishes' flank. They circled her, swimming slowly, stalking their prey.

"Fuck you," Nadia screamed, kicking out as best she could.

The water offered a healthy resistance, removing all power from her blow. Her foot hit one of the creatures, but it did nothing but further irritate the beast.

Nadia stumbled, losing her footing as the fish closed in around her feet. The water reached waist deep. She looked back, noticing the ship's rear still rose out of the water. Nadia realized she stood no chance of surviving, but reaching higher ground would buy her some time. A few precious moments of life.

Half-running, half-swimming, Nadia hauled herself out of the water. She scaled the wall, the ship now almost vertical in the water. The equipment racks made an effective ladder. Once free, Nadia pulled herself to her feet and looked around. Lights dotted the horizon. A boat, a few of them. Too far away to save her. Not that she had any means of contacting them.

Something crashed against the ship, and Nadia fell. One moment she stood in relative safety, the next she hit the water and disappeared beneath the surface.

Fish surrounded her. Even with her hazy vision, she could make out their numbers. They circled, swimming in close to take a small bite, a sample.

Sharp teeth tore into her flesh, puncture wounds and bite marks that filled the ocean with blood. Nadia struggled, her lungs burning as her body demanded air. She kicked and thrashed, but could not make her way to the surface. The mass of fish held her down. They came in groups now, snatching at her flesh. They were smaller fish, albeit ones two or three times larger than the species should grow.

Nadia was dead long before the big brothers moved in and tore her body apart in a frenzy.

The *Amity Three* slid beneath the surface of the ocean. The waters calmed, and the night returned to its normal peaceful state.

CHAPTER 4

Melissa Stone closed her laptop and let out a long, slow sigh. She sat back in her chair and her back gave an audible crack. Melissa stretched and rubbed her eyes. She looked at the clock and groaned. Two in the morning always came too quickly. The alarm was set to sound in little over three hours.

In the corner of the small room, her home office in the back of her three-bedroom home, two suitcases sat, swollen with holiday clothes.

The long overdue break would be the first holiday Melissa had taken since her divorce. She did not know who was more excited. Her, or her daughter, Rachel.

The divorce had been hard on Rachel. While her parents remained friendly, the split was not one driven by extra marital affairs or any seedy business, but simply through years of separation and the dwindling feeling of love.

Melissa was a reporter for a large national paper. She did not write the headline pieces, but her articles were always well received. She worked long hours, and while a lot of the time she could work from home, the drain on her was inevitable.

With her last article submitted, Melissa was ready to enjoy the coming ten days with her daughter. They had chosen the resort together. Melissa had fallen in love with the white sand beaches and the idea of being so far away from the rest of the world. Rachel loved the look of the Kids' Klub and the activities they offered. They both loved the idea of snorkeling along the reef, which had been constructed by the resort and was home to all manner of sea life.

Melissa got up from the table and moved through into the kitchen. Melissa knew that if she did not grab at least a few hours of sleep then she would never survive the trip. Melissa could never get to sleep when flying. Not through fear, but simply because she never found a comfortable enough position, and her finances did not stretch enough to accommodate first-class travel.

Moving through the house, she checked to ensure everything they would not need in the morning was turned off, and wherever possible, unplugged. It only left her with the coffee pot and the toaster. They had plans to eat a real breakfast at the airport before they boarded the plane, but a piece of toast and a cup of coffee were a must before leaving the house.

Melissa moved upstairs, stopping in the doorway to Rachel's room. She pushed the door open and peered through the room. Rachel slept soundly, buried under her duvet and a pile of pillows. The nightlight by her bed filled the room with a comforting glow. Melissa thought about turning the illuminated cartoon character off. She decided against it. A fear of the dark was nothing to worry about, and if her daughter slept better with a night light, then so be it. Her (now) ex-husband had been very forceful on the issue of fears and did not believe in letting them win.

Melissa's room was at the end of the hallway. The room between them was empty. Technically a guest room, Melissa had often talked about creating a home gym, but she knew a money-wasting idea when she heard one. Although, she was not getting any younger, and certain areas she once considered pert and perky were becoming noticeably less so as time moved on. Plus, in all the time they lived in the house, the guest room had yet to be used. She agreed with her conscience that she would think about the idea while relaxing in Mexico.

Sliding into bed, Melissa settled down on her side. Even though they finalized their divorce close to two years before, Melissa still found herself sleeping on her side of the bed. She tried sleeping in the middle, she tried sleeping on the other side, but each time her sleep was disrupted. Melissa liked her side of the bed, and when the need arose, Rachel always knew she had a place to crawl if she got scared.

Melissa fell asleep quickly, tumbling into the restful black. The dreams that awaited her were less restful.

The house was dark; the hallways seemed to go on and on, offering corners that led onto more hallways and corners, an endless loop. The red-painted walls were faded, paint peeled away in large flakes. The shit-coloured brown came with a matching odour. It hung in the air; stale and foul, like a portable toilet left flushed and uncleaned. The stench was cloying, and lined every breath, coating the inside of Melissa's mouth and nose. She pulled her shirt up over her mouth, but even that could not keep out the lingering essence of excrement.

Behind her, something moved, an echo of footsteps and heavy breathing. Melissa spun around. A mist filled the hallways, rolling towards her like a storm. She turned again, to run, but a similar cloud of mist approached from the other side. Floating high, moving from a dense white cloud by the ceiling, clearing to nothing down by the floor. Melissa had to move, but her feet were heavy, the mist holding her body in place.

Grunting, Melissa forced her legs to move, to walk. The mist grabbed at her, but she found that movement made its grip weak.

She walked as quickly as the mist allowed. A corner to the left drew closer. She heard a laugh, a cracked, growling sound, more like a cackle, which faded as Melissa rounded the corner. At the end of the hall, stood an enormous hulking figure. Too large to be a man yet, it stood on two legs. Something dangled from the thing's hands. A long hard rod, straight until the large bulbous head swelled at one end.

Melissa recognized the weapon as a hammer, a sledgehammer. The thing didn't move, but the mist swirled around the form, enveloping it.

Behind her something groaned. Melissa turned as a shape formed in the swirling mist. A crocodile, its long snout open, exposing rotting, yellowed teeth set in blooding gums. The croc walked toward Melissa, its scaled body shimmering in the haze. The mouth closed and the groaning sound came again. The thick body shuddered.

The beast was crying, weeping as the mist settled on its massive head, condensing to fall as fake tears. The sound was not laden with grief, but filled with a mocking sarcasm, a slow weep which gave the impression of only ever being a slight change away from becoming a laugh.

Melissa wanted to run, but she couldn't. Long tendrils of mist had sunk down, reached for her. They curled around her ankles, forming shackles that locked her in place.

A loud scraping sound made her spin around. The figure was back, its hammer dragging along the floor as the beast made its way closer to her. The nearer it drew, the more its form took shape. The hulking figure was covered from head to toe in matted brown fur, which fell from the body in mangy clumps, exposing black, putrid flesh beneath.

The lips pulled back, receding into the stubby snout revealing teeth even more terrifying than those of the crocodile, which continued to weep behind her.

The bear raised its head and sniffed at the air, before returning its gaze to Melissa. She gasped, for the bear's eyes were starting to glow, a flickering orange, like two dancing flames. The bear heaved the sledgehammer into the air and roared.

The hammer swung, Melissa screamed, her voice rising to drown out the bear. Her scream engulfed everything, pulling Melissa back to wakefulness. She sat upright in her bed, breathing heavy, the sound of terror still ringing out around her.

Rachel was screaming. Her cries cut through the dream and through the darkness. Melissa sprang out of bed and sprinted into her daughter's room.

Rachel sat upright in bed, clutching her covers up to her chin. Melissa turned on the light and Rachel jumped. The dream held her from waking fully, but the light chased it away.

"Mum … mum … I was being attacked by a giant shark," Rachel panted, fearing having chased the breath from her lungs.

For a moment, Melissa imagined her daughter saying bear rather than shark. "Honey, it was just a bad dream. Do you want to come and sleep next to me?" Melissa asked, rubbing her eyes. She waited a few moments before rising. Being pulled from deep sleep, combined with her nightmare, left her unsteady on her feet.

"Yes, please." Rachel threw her covers to one side and climbed out of bed.

As she moved, a book fell from within the thick duvet and clattered onto the floor. Melissa bent down to pick it up. "Now I wonder, what on earth could have given you that bad dream?" She held up the copy of *Jaws* and gave her daughter a stern look.

"Sorry, Mum, but everybody says it is such a great book." Rachel was always willing to argue her case. A ten year old going on twenty-one.

"Who is everybody? I certainly never recommended this as a good book." Melissa knew she could not win the conversation, but she needed to play the parent card, and at least throw a modicum of conviction into the performance.

"Ugh, Goodreads, Mum. That's where everybody is." At any other time of day, the statement would have been followed up by a roll of the eyes and possible a petulant sigh, but at such an ungodly hour, words alone would suffice.

"Oh, now I understand, how stupid of me. Well, come on, let's get back to bed. The alarm goes soon and I really want to get some rest."

The pair headed back to bed, and slept soundly until the shrill beep of the ever increasingly annoyed alarm shattered the silence of sleep.

***

The trip was uneventful. Rachel had been entertained by the kid's channel on the plane's in-flight entertainment system, and against all odds, Melissa managed to sleep, for the first time in her life.

They landed mid-morning, and a bus was waiting to take them to the new resort. It was located off the coast, and only accessible by a small private ferryboat.

While the plane leg of their journey went smooth, the bus proved to be a different matter. Hot and overcrowded, the air conditioning did little to combat the heat of the day. Rachel got remarkably car sick, and spent the whole trip with her head in her mother's lap, her skin turning a more impressive shade of green with every mile they travelled.

She reached the resort without throwing up, which Melissa counted as a win.

The resort was beautiful, almost more so than the pictures on their website.

The sun was shining and the sky was a cloudless blue, as deep a shade as Melissa had ever seen. The staff all wore dazzlingly white uniforms; the women were petite and had smiles spread over their faces. Real smiles, not the fake kind so often offered by those in the hospitality business. The men were all tanned the same deep bronze shade, and muscular.

Melissa felt more relaxed than she could remember being in a long time. At the very least, the eye candy on offer stood to make her trip a success.

Check-in was quick and painless. They got the keys to their chalet and a map to help them find it. The resort was split between a hotel building and a number of holiday homes. Closely grouped, they spread across the whole island resort.

Melissa booked with the request to be placed near a pool, but away from the hotel. She got both her wishes. The series of houses she and Rachel walked towards came with their own private pool. Set in the middle of the small cul-de-sac of buildings, it immediately caught Rachel's attention. There were no slides or diving boards, no vendors selling snack food, and certainly no cocktail bar, just a simple pool that would keep Rachel occupied while they were at the chalet. It was perfect.

Most of their time would be spent out by the bigger, busier areas, but the pool gave Melissa the freedom to start the day at a slower pace, with a coffee and a good book, while her daughter played.

"Mum, can I go swimming?" Rachel asked almost the second they crossed the chalet's threshold.

"Okay, grab your swimsuit and put on some sunscreen," Melissa answered. "And stick to this pool for now, okay?"

"Sure thing, Mum," Rachel shrieked excitedly as she tore into her suitcase in search of her swimming suit. She had brought three; two one pieces and a bikini-style set. She grabbed the first one she came across, squealed and hurriedly dressed, disappearing before Melissa even had the chance to place her first suitcase on the bed. Rachel had the pool to herself, but unlike Melissa, Rachel never had a problem finding and making friends.

Melissa unpacked and looked around the house. Despite being an all-inclusive resort, the houses came with a small kitchen area. It did not have an oven or anything like that, but tea and coffee supplies, a sink and a small refrigerator still made a small kitchenette.

"Hey, Rachel," Melissa called. "Rachel, come on in and dry off, we're going to take a look around."

Rachel came at the first time of asking.

The man-made island was surrounded on all sides by white sandy beaches. A series of small electronic trains ran in a continue loop bringing people to and from the beaches. The end of the island was only a ten or fifteen-minute walk away, for a family, but Melissa had no plans to walk the entire resort. Reading the brochures, and watching the introduction video that was playing on the TV in the living room, told her enough about the farther reaches of the island.

The resort boasted seven restaurants, each offering a different variety of good food, and only one of which required bookings and came with a one visit per week policy. A litany of smaller food stalls stood across the grounds, severing everything from grilled cheese and pancakes to Mexican snack foods.

The main reception area and hotel were on the northern tip, with a private stretch of beach reserved for hotel guests. There were three main recreation areas, with multiple pools for guests of all ages. Water slides rose in clusters, like three-dimensional Snakes and Ladders boards. Sun loungers and hammocks were positioned everywhere, and large patches of grass were filled with sunbathers and kids playing everything from football to Frisbee.

Multiple bars surrounded them, offering drinks from across the globe, soft drinks, beers, wines and spirits, all of them included in the cost of the stay. The resort lived up to its claims of being a veritable paradise on earth. Just walking around and taking in the sights was enough for Melissa to unwind and relax.

"Mum, can we sign me up for the Kids' Klub? I really want to go," Rachel said, tugging on her mother's arm as they walked by the large play area and the signs advertising the kids' activity center.

"Okay, but I think they are closed now," Melissa said, looking through the playground at the building in the background.

"Can we go check, please?" Rachel begged.

"Okay, we can take a quick look. Otherwise, I promise we will come back tomorrow," Melissa said and Rachel set off before she finished talking.

The 'Klub House' was empty, leaving Rachel clearly disappointed, but the promise of another swim in the main pool, and her choice of restaurant for dinner soon turned the frown upside down. The resort was new, in the middle of its first summer. As such, everything still had the lingering air of total luxury. The plants were new, the grass still lush and green, with no sign of prolonged use by sun-sloths and rambunctious children.

"What do you say we check out the beach, have a swim in the ocean? I bet the ocean is lovely and warm," Melissa offered Rachel the choice.

"Okay, but if I see a shark, I'm out of there," Rachel answered with all the seriousness a ten-year-old can muster.

"Sure thing," Melissa answered just as serious.

"I am serious, Mum. Those things are monsters. They think we are seals and just eat you."

"I don't think sharks eat that many people, but if you spot one in the swimming area, we will go to the pool," Melissa said, offering the alternative quickly, before Rachel found time to spout some shark attack statistic.

The beach was crowded directly in front of the hotel area, but for those willing to walk an extra minute or two, the long stretch of white sand offered plenty of quieter spots.

"Oh look at that," Melissa called, coming to a stop in front of a large hand-painted sign.

"Really? Scuba diving?" Rachel looked at her mother.

"Yeah, why not? I love the ocean, and I always wanted to learn how to dive." Melissa found herself defending her choices to her daughter. "Besides, look at the times. You will be in your Kids' Klub thing then, so I can go and do this, when we can spend the afternoon together."

"Okay, but if a shark makes you its lunch or something, don't say I didn't try to stop you."

"Well, technically you haven't tried to stop me, and second of all, there are no killer sharks around this resort. I promise you."

"No, no sharks, not killer anyway. Sharks are one of the most beautiful things in the sea, young miss," a voice spoke up. A few moments later, the owner appeared from behind the sign.

Melissa guessed the man to be in his early forties. He wore a bright red, unbuttoned shirt, which flapped behind him like a cape as he walked. He also had on a pair of brightly coloured swimming shorts. His bare feet sunk into the sand. Clearly in good shape, the muscles of his exposed chest, and abs had the look of a man who took care of himself. Toned but not bulky.

"My name is Raul. I teach the diving courses her at the resort. Are you interested in booking a lesson or two?" he asked, offering his hand as he spoke. His accent had a different air to it than the other members of staff they had met.

"Oh, I am not sure. I've never tried diving before. I mean, it does look like fun, but ... how much do they cost?"

"The first few lessons are one hundred US, that includes everything you need. After that, well, it depends on how much of a natural you are. If you wanted, I offer a full certification for one-fifty, and run diving trips further out, for fifty bucks a trip," Raul answered.

"That's a lot of money, Mum," Rachel spoke up.

"Actually, honey, that is very reasonable," Rachel answered her daughter. "Can we have a trial lesson tomorrow morning? If I like it, then maybe I will book the whole course."

"Of course, what time would suit you?" Raul asked. His eyes seemed to glint as he smiled.

"Let's say eleven ... no wait, ten-thirty. That would be best."

"Sure thing. Meet me back here tomorrow at around ten-fifteen, if you can, then we can get everything set up and make the most of the time in the water." The smile on Raul's face seemed genuine, his interest in diving and getting people out into the water shone through.

"Great, see you then."

CHAPTER 5

Manuel Espinoza and Santiago Castillo stood on the deck of the privately owned tuna fishing boat. The end of a long day loomed on the horizon. They lost two big Bluefin, one in the morning and one in the early afternoon. Manuel's mood swung between grumpy and resigned.

"Where the heck are the fish?" Manuel asked rhetorically.

"No idea, chief, but they are not here," Santiago answered. He was a man who took things are literally as anybody could take them.

A damned fine fisherman and a grafter unlike anybody Santiago had seen before, he earned his money and then some on board Santiago's ship, the *Blue Fin.*

"Hey, Rey, do you have anything on the sonar yet?" Santiago called up to his first mate. Rey Delgado was a heavy set man with forearms the size of a man's upper arm, which on Rey were the size of a normal man's thigh. With an equally impressive belly, and more tattoos than bare skin left on his upper body, he cut an imposing figure. He was a hulking brute of a man, and the gentlest soul Santiago had ever met.

The men had worked together for five years, fishing for tuna and running private hire fishing trips when necessary. Manuel was the new member of the group, having joined six months earlier.

"No, I don't know what's happened, but the targets that were there disappeared," Rey called back down, his head appearing above the railings. Sweat glistened on his bald head.

"I don't understand, we were right on them," Santiago said as he climbed the ladder up to the wheelhouse.

"We were, a damned big group of them, but what can I tell you, they just vanished. Maybe they sunk down deep so that we couldn't find them," Rey offered.

"I doubt it, they ain't never done something like that before."

"No, but they also ain't never disappeared from the sonar either, chief," Rey answered, wiping his brow with a handkerchief.

"Boss man, you need to see this," Manuel called from the boat.

Both Santiago and Rey looked down from the wheelhouse. They didn't need Manuel to explain why he called them. The rich blue of the ocean was gone. The water was stained red with blood.

The red patch spread like an oil slick. Chunks of flesh bobbed on the water like ice cubes in a Bloody Mary.

"What on earth?" Rey said, taking off his sunglasses to squint at the spreading mass.

"I guess we know what happened to the tuna," Santiago said.

Below them, on the deck, Manuel made the sign of the cross over his chest, and leaned over the edge of the craft to take a closer look.

The fish leaped from the water, breaching like a hunting whale. Its mouth opened and it engulfed Manuel as the fish began the downward turn of its leap. The monster seemed to be more teeth than fish, the mouth hyperextending in order to create a gap between the upper and lower jaws. They snapped closed with a wet smack. Manuel exploded with a pop, blood and entrails spurting from his body, leaking from around the fish's lips.

The fish was at least six feet long. Landing on the deck with an almighty crash, the impact crushing the deck, the fish proceeded to smash the siding as it thrashed its muscular body. The deck filled with blood, which flooded from the remaining half of Manuel's body. Thick strings of intestine, bloated and blue in the light of day, snaked over the deck, floating on the tide of blood.

The boat listed to starboard as the giant fish slid through the dismantled siding and into the ocean.

Manuel's lower half followed suit, falling into the water with a hollow plop. The two remaining men stood in shocked silence up in the wheelhouse.

"What the hell was that?" Rey asked, rubbing his shoulder from where he had fallen against the boat's controls when the fish crashed into his boat.

"Beats me, but there are more, look." Santiago pointed into the ocean just beyond the *Blue Fin*. It was teeming with fish that tore at Manuel's remains, shearing flesh from bone, adding a pinkish froth to the red-stained ocean.

"We need to get out of here. Push the motors into the redline," Santiago said.

"Already on it," Rey replied. "Something is wrong; I'm not getting any power from the engines."

"What do you mean?" Santiago asked. He never got to hear the answer, because in the next moment, the something crashed against the boat with enough force to lift the hull out of the water and send the craft tumbling over to the starboard side. Santiago and Rey both plunged into the savage, infested water.

Santiago kicked his way to the surface, trying to ignore the pain as the fish began to nibble at him. He could feel them, hundreds of them taking bites of out of his flesh. His mind wanted to shut down, the pain was so intense. Santiago didn't need to look down to understand that one of the bigger creatures had taken his leg off at the knee. Not that he would have seen anything if he had changed the glance. The water around him turned an even richer shade of red as his blood added to the discolouration already present.

Across from him, Santiago stared as Rey hauled himself up and onto the hull of the overturned boat. His back was torn apart, the flesh stripped away to reveal the bone beneath. He was missing a foot on his right leg while blood poured from a wound on his abdomen. The blood made the hull slick. The more frantic Rey became as he struggled to maintain his grip, the more blood he lost, and the faster he slid back into the water.

A white hot pain erupted in Santiago's belly. The impact of the fish pushed him through the water. Teeth burrowed deep into his gut. The force pulled him beneath the surface. Pain exploded in him as Santiago reached out and grabbed the fish with both hands. It thrashed and squirmed against him. He pulled, kicking with his remaining leg as other fish nibbled at him.

The larger fish squirmed of out his grip and bit down on Santiago's hand, shearing it from the arm in a single bite. Screaming beneath the waves, water flooded his throat. His suffering ended when the large fish attached again, snapping its toothy maw shut around his face. Long teeth pierced his skull and skewered his brain. The front part of his head was yanked clear from the rest of his skull with a powerful jerk.

On the boat, Rey managed to pull himself into a position that brought his whole body raised up, out of the water. He held on with one hand, using his other arm to cradle his belly, which had been split from left to right. Thick rolls of yellow fat spilled from his stomach, dragging with them strands of intestine that hung from the smile-shaped gash like wagging tongues.

The fish broke the water with a splash, the size of a large great white shark. The giant body breached and came crashing down on the boat, flattening the dying Rey. *Don't let them eat my eyes,* Rey's final thought shot through his head before his body exploded under the weight of the giant fish.

CHAPTER 6

Troy got off the plane and stretched. He was worn out. His flight had been delayed by four and a half hours, and he had been seated behind an American who insisted on spending the whole flight lying down, his seat back fully reclined, leaving Troy somewhat pinned to his chair.

Luckily for him, the head steward turned out to be a fan of MMA and recognized Troy from his last few fights. He managed to arrange a better seat, no upgrade, but a better seat. It was great to be off the plane. Even though he was stiff and sweaty, he was eager to escape the airport and head out into the sun.

Collecting his bags, Troy followed the signs to where the coach that would take them to the ferry that leads to the resort, sat waiting.

He loudly cursed his luck when the same American from the plane appeared two places ahead of him in the queue for the bus. The gods were in his favour, however, when the man squeezed his large frame into one of the seats at the front of the coach. Troy purposefully chose a seat towards the rear as a result.

The trip was a simple one. Troy fell asleep wedged into his window seat, and woke up as they drove onto the ferry. His chin was wet with drool, and from the look his large-framed seat buddy shot his way, he would guess snoring had been an issue also.

Troy moved away from the group as the ferry set sail. He stood on the far side, gazing out into the ocean. The hot air was kept cool by the ocean breeze. He loved the water, always had. From the sea to pool, rivers and lakes, as a kid, growing up, Troy would swim in any body of water he came across.

Looking down into the water, Troy caught sight of something moving just beneath the surface. A long back broke the surface, the body curving round to disappear back beneath the surface too quick to afford him a real glance.

Troy kept his eyes on the water as another form appeared, and another. Their sightings were equally brief, and while some part of his brain was alarmed, he reasoned to himself that they must have been dolphins. A group of young dolphins following the boat. He had read about that happening.

When the boat rocked suddenly, just a few moments later, Troy paid it no mind. Slowly, Troy's mind wandered back to the water, and the horizon.

The resort staff welcomed them all with flair, a peppy and infectious hype. Smiling as he walked, Troy hummed a made-up tune as he walked over to his cabin, located towards the southern side of the resort. Troy made the request as he checked in, not wanting to be stuck against the hotel. The idea of a little privacy was an appealing concept.

He unpacked his bags, and looked around the house-style chalet. With two floors and two bedrooms, the place offered more space than he would need. The small private pool offered an additional bonus Tory had not been expecting. An older couple lay stretched out on the sun loungers, their skin a deep, dark bronze. They did not move once between Troy's arrival and his re-emergence after unpacking his belongings.

Changing out of his jeans and T-shirt, Troy jumped into a pair of swimming shorts and a shirt emblazoned with the name of his sponsor. Even when on vacation, a little bit of marketing went a long way.

Making his way back towards the main pool area, Troy paused to watch a volleyball game down on the beach. The women playing sucked at the sport, and clearly didn't understand the rules, but nobody seemed too interested in telling them.

He moved away after a moment, and settled down on a stool near a bar, choosing a seat close to the water, under the shade of a large palm tree.

A waiter came by to take his order, a move which surprised and delighted him. Troy looked over the menu and went to order a beer, but then he realized he was on holiday, and chose a cocktail that sounded like a move out of the Karma Sutra, and contained more types of spirit than he knew existed.

The sun was hot, even in the shade its power was clear. Troy drank his drink and read his book, feeling better by the minute.

"Can I get you another one, sir?" the same friendly waiter asked.

"Yes, yes please. I'll have the same again," Troy answered.

The man walked away, and Troy slid off his chair, lowering himself into the pool. The water was cool, but not as cold as he expected. The mushroom-shaped pool had a circular head forming the main swimming area. The stalk had a bench-style seat running along the edges. There were a few people in the pool, including a couple with a young baby. Troy smiled at them. They smiled back, and the baby gave a giggled cry as she splashed the water with both of her pudgy arms. The water was cool, and Troy pushed himself down beneath the surface. The silence swept over him like a surging tide. Through the water, Troy could make out the hazy forms of the others in the pool, but for the most part, he felt completely isolated. The world no longer existed once he disappeared beneath the surface.

He held his breath until his lungs hurt, enjoying the peace, and also enjoying the burn. Ever since he was a kid, he and his brother would compete to see who could hold their breath the longest. Troy won, every single time.

Breaking the surface, Troy saw that the couple with the baby were staring at him, their faces etched with concern. Troy smiled at them and jumped out of the pool. His drink was waiting for him. Taking a long sip, he lay back, and fell asleep.

He woke a while later, refreshed and ready for the day. It by mid-afternoon, the intense heat of midday had passed and a delightful warmth took its place. The pool seemed busier. A few kids appeared, chasing each other and jumping into the main swimming area. Their shrieks and laughs were loud, but far from irritating.

The family with the baby were gone, but several people now sat on the pool benches, drinks in hand. They were talking and laughing. Troy noticed a young woman sitting facing him. While she sat close to the others, there could be no mistaking she did not belong to their group. She made no attempt to join their conversations, either. She just sat in the water, her head raised to the sky. Troy could not take his eyes off her pale, fair skin and long brunette hair. She was without doubt, an attractive woman. Troy also sensed she was intensely lonely. Just as he contemplated ordering another drink and sliding into the pool, with the intention of striking up a conversation with somebody who looked like they needed it, the woman's daughter arrived and pulled her mother's attention away.

The woman climbed out of the pool, her deep blue bikini clinging to her slender curves, and disappeared, chasing after her daughter.

Troy got up and stretched. His stomach growled, and with a satisfied sigh, he set off in search of food.

Troy was lucky as far as maintaining his weight. He fought at a natural weight, which meant he had room to play with in terms of gains during his off-duty periods. Not that his weight ever fluctuated too much. Troy liked to eat, and he loved to train, so even when he didn't have a fight planned, his training remained just as intensive, all be it with a different focus.

Troy spent the rest of the afternoon exploring the resort, concentrating on the beaches to the south, away from the general population. He went for a swim, then took a gentle jog along the beach. The weather was beautiful and Troy followed the beach around the resort back to his chalet. The slow descending sun cast a beautiful late afternoon glow over everything.

Troy returned to his chalet, showered and dressed. He had already seen the restaurant where he planned on having dinner. You could never go wrong with Chinese food.

Sitting in the chalet's small front terrace, Troy relaxed, watching the world go by. He almost jumped when the bikini-clad woman from the pool walked out of the front door of the chalet next to him.

She came out and sat down at the small garden table. She had changed since the pool, choosing to wear a light navy blue summer dress with a white ribbon tied around the waist.

A few moments later, her daughter emerged and jumped straight into the pool. The woman gave a sigh.

"Bad day?" Troy asked, seizing the opportunity to speak to the stranger. Recalling the way she looked in the pool, as if she just needed somebody to sit down and offer her some company.

The woman looked around sharply, managing to stifle the surprised jump. "Oh, no not at all. I just, well, you don't want to hear it." She caught herself staring at the man and lowered her gaze.

"Oh, I don't mind. It's kind of quiet sitting here alone." Troy waited for her reaction. She looked up as he spoke, her eyes finding his once more.

"It can be," she said without thinking. "I had a scuba diving lesson booked for tomorrow, but it just got cancelled, or well, pushed out another day." Troy detected a slight blush on her cheeks.

"That's a shame. Have you never gone diving before?" he asked.

"No, I've always wanted to try though."

"Oh, it is wonderful. Being out in the water, so far away from everything."

"You scuba dive?" she asked, trying not to sound surprised.

"Yes, I do, well, I did. Not been out in the water for a while," Toy answered, adjusting his seat so he sat facing the woman.

"It must be nice," she said.

"Oh, it's wonderful. I have a kind of crazy life, and getting into the water, disappearing beneath the waves, there is nothing better." Troy stopped talking. He noticed the woman staring at him.

"I know you," she said, blushing.

"I have one of those faces," Troy lied.

"No, no, I know you. My ex-husband was a huge fan of that cage fighting, and you, you fought a lot, but I cannot remember you name," the woman talked faster and faster as she attempted to hide her embarrassment at not being able to name a perfect stranger.

"Troy, Troy Deane," he said with a smile, leaning over the small wall between the properties, offering his hand.

"That's right. They call you Bomber, right?" she spoke with a smile.

"Yes, good memory," Troy said.

"My name is Melissa Stone, it's nice to meet you," Melissa smiled coyly.

"Nice to meet you, Melissa. I don't want to sound forward or anything, but if your scuba lesson has been cancelled, why don't I take you snorkelling tomorrow? Out on the reef to the south of the resort?" Troy asked, making a bold move, but he was on holiday, meeting people belonged to the experience, and, truth be told, he liked the idea of having some company during his break.

"Oh, I don't know. I mean, I have my daughter here, and well, I don't really know you," Melissa stammered.

"Oh, hey, no pressure. Just a friendly thing, no hidden strings or anything like that. Besides, if she wants to hang with the old people, your daughter can come along too. The more the merrier." Troy sat back and took a drink of his water.

"You know what, to hell with it. I'd love to. Rachel, that's my daughter, has this Kids' Klub thing tomorrow, so shall I meet you here at say, ten-thirty?"

Melissa rose from the table and sat perched on the low wall. Her eyes locked on Troy's and held them for a few moments.

"That sounds great, I'll meet you here tomorrow. Now, you will have to excuse me, I am famished." Troy rose and patted his belly.

"Oh, of course. Have a good night, Mr. Deane." Melissa rose also, and as Troy walked away toward the restaurant, he cast a glance over his shoulder. Melissa was busy trying to coax her daughter out of the water.

CHAPTER 7

Antonio shut off the ignition to his beat-up old Ford and sat in silence. The only sound was the ticking of the engine as it cooled. It looked as though the others were no shows. Beside him, his best friend Mark shuffled in his seat.

"Are we sure this is the place?" he asked.

"Yes, this is where we met last time too," Antonio answered. "They will be here. Maria is never on time for things. She'd be late to her own funeral. Let's go get ready."

The men left the car and walked down to the beach. The small bay created a secluded paradise that very few people knew about. Their buddy Lopez found it the summer before, and since nobody else ever came down, they claimed it as their own private spot. The waves were not necessarily the best on the coast, but the bay offered a nice swell and fast breaks that made for a fun afternoon with friends.

Not long after they got to the beach, they recognized the familiar rumble of Lopez's old Volkswagen. The car was a health hazard, and how any authority allowed it to stay on the roads was mind-boggling.

The faces of their friend, and his long-time girlfriend Maria, appeared above them. Smiling and waving frantically, the pair raced down to the beach, a third friend hurrying behind them.

"Welcome back, guys." Lopez exchanged a round of high-fives with his friends. "It's been too long."

"Tell me about it. I wanted to come up earlier, but school just fucked me up last semester," Antonio joked.

"You guys remember Maria, right?" The introduction being an in-joke with the group, as Mark introduced Lopez to Maria, one of his oldest friends, three years before.

"I think I remember you mentioning her," Mark said, embracing Maria in a big hug.

"I've missed you guys," she said with a smile. "I brought a friend with me too. Chlöe, these are the guys I told you about last night." Maria beckoned her friend to join them. "She's single, too." Maria looked at Mark as she spoke, slipping him a quick wink.

"Hi." Chlöe waved as she moved into the group.

They chatted a while, until everybody became painfully aware of Maria's intentions to couple Mark and her friend. The water soon called them, and they grabbed their boards and headed into the ocean.

Antonio and Lopez ran in first, with Chlöe just behind them. Maria and Mark remained on the beach for a moment.

"You like her," Maria said, smiling.

"I'd be stupid not to," Mark answered, looking at one of his oldest friends. "She's stunning."

Mark looked at the shapely blonde paddling out into the water. Her shoulder-length hair and green eyes had captured his heart in an instant. Her curves and athletic frame have her a stunning appeal, a joyful sexiness that was already starting to tug at his soul.

"Then go get her, tiger." Maria slapped Mark on the back as he ran into the water, his board raised above his head.

"So, how long have you known Maria?" Chlöe asked as she sat astride her board.

She and Mark drifted a little distance away from the others in their group, but neither seemed over bothered by it.

"Oh, we go way back. Back to high school. I've known her longer than Antonio. I met him in the first month of college," Mark answered

"Cool, so you trust her?"

"Of course, why?"

"Well, if you trust her, then I trust her, and she said that you and I would be a good match." Chlöe smiled, and her eyes twinkled

"Well, I would trust her with my life," Mark said, reaching out to place his hand on top of Chlöe's.

She smiled at him.

"Ow, sonofabitch," she cried out, jerking her body on the board. "Sorry, something just bit my toe."

"Lopez said there would be fish in the bay," Mark said, looking around the water, nervous.

"Yeah, but I didn't know they would bite. It really stings too." The real extent of the pain brimmed in Chlöe's eyes. Tears welling, ready to fall the moment he looked away.

"Here, let me take a look, make sure it is nothing serious." Mark slapped his hand on his own board. "Swing your leg up here."

Chlöe pulled her leg out of the water, her upper body not moving as she raised the limb out of the water and placed it on the surfboard.

Her foot was covered in blood. Her big toe was missing, severed clean off her foot.

The blood flowed from the blood stump, like lava spilling from a volcano. Unable to hold back her anguish any longer, Chlöe opened her mouth and screamed. An ear-piercing cry. With her blood staining the water pink, fish began circling them. Flecks of bright blue light flickered into and out of view beneath the surface, like neon lights trying hard to sustain enough energy to remain alight.

Behind them, another cry rang out. Mark turned his head as a large fish leap out of the water, its large jaws stretched back to reveal a mouth full of large teeth. The jaws snapped shut around Maria's throat. The weight of the fish tore the flesh free with a shower of blood. The body twisted and fell back into the water, leaving Maria sitting on her board, as if unaware anything had happened.

Maria remained sitting, blood pumping from her throat like vomit, chumming the sea. With a look of total confusion plastered to her face, she slid from her board and instantly disappeared beneath the surface.

"We need to get back to shore. Can you paddle?" Mark asked frantic, conscious of the swirl of activity from whatever creatures were lurking beneath the surface and the danger they presented.

"Yes, I think so," Chlöe replied, crying. The blood loss caused her face to pale, but her eyes still held a look of steely determination.

The pair began to paddle back to shore, while a short way over, their friends were trying to do the same.

The water around Lopez and Antonio came alive. It bubbled as if boiling, and as the two men tried to break free, the fish attacked.

Water spouted up around them, combining with the blood to create a crimson and white fountain of foaming gore. Antonio screamed and thrashed. One creature leaped clear of the water, its jaws clamping down on Antonio's arm, teeth sinking through the flesh as if it were nothing. The power of the crushing jaws snapped the bone and tore the remaining strands of connective tissue free with a savage wrench of its body.

Lopez surged passed, paddling for all he was worth. His foot was missing, reduced to nothing more than a bloody stump with a fractured stalk of bone protruding down to the point where the ankle should begin.

Something pulled at Mark below the water, tugging his whole body sideways. Pain exploded in his leg, the same agonizing sensation as waking in the dead of night with a cramp in his calf, only magnified tenfold.

He held in his scream and continued to kick, pushing his underwater attacker away with a final desperate shot. Chlöe was next to him. A fish leaped from the water and landed on her back. It was about two feet long and thrashed around, struggling with being out of the water, and unable to use its jaws to find purchase on the tender flesh it sought. Mark sat up a way, reached over, and grabbed the thing by the tail. He picked it up, noticing the long-hanging, barb-like appendage that descended from beneath the lower jaw. The end thrashed and buried itself in Chlöe's back, hooking into the skin. Mark almost lost his grip on the fish as its body contracted, in an attempt to pull itself down towards its captured prey.

Mark grunted and heaved the fish into the air. The barb tore free from Chlöe's back with a bloody plop. Mark hurled the fish over his shoulder, and it crashed back into the sea a few meters behind them.

"We need to hurry," he gasped, the pain ripping through his leg and lower body starting to take its toll. His blood turning the waters around him darker and darker.

"Mark, help," Antonio's voice called out. Mark turned to see his friend in the water. His surfboard was broken, the two halves bouncing around in the water as the creatures attacked it for good measure.

"Keep paddling. Get to the shore," Mark instructed Chlöe.

"You can't go back for him," she cried.

"He's my best friend," Mark said.

Turning his board around, Mark beat a fast pace towards his friend. Antonio was struggling in the water, trying hard to stay on the surface.

"Here, give me your hand," Mark called, holding out his arm. His hand found Antonio's outstretched grip, and he pulled. His friend's body seemed light in the water.

"Grab my board, pull yourself up," Mark called out, already starting to manoeuver himself for a run back to the shore.

Antonio made no move to pull himself clear, and as Mark heaved, helping his friend out of the water, he understood why. Antonio's lower half was missing. Thick coils of intestines dangled from his severed waist like octopus' tentacles. Mark screamed. He looked at his friend, but Antonio was dead. Blood dribbled from his mouth, and his wide eyes bulged in their sockets. Mark let him go and immediately the body dipped beneath the surface.

Mark started to paddle back, buoyed on by the sight of Chlöe pulling herself out of the surf and onto the beach, the minced meat stump at the end of her leg leaving a bloody trail on the wet sand.

Ahead of him, Mark searched the water for Lopez. There was no sign of his body, the remains of his board floating unoccupied on the waves.

Mark moved past the board, the shore was close. Chloe sat up in the sand, screaming his name over and over.

Whatever it was, hit the surfboard from underneath, impacting with enough force to snap the board in half, lifting Mark clean out of the water. He looked down to find the ugly brown face of a creature straight out of a nightmare, staring back up at him.

Time slowed, and as he began to fall, Mark prepared himself for the hungry jaws waiting for him.

He crashed into the water, his body an agonized song of pain and fear. He kicked to the surface. His board forgotten, Mark began to swim. The water grew shallow. His hands scratched the sand, and he tried to scramble to his feet. Pain exploded and Mark's legs gave out beneath him. He fell beneath the water and the fish attacked. Two latched onto his legs, and another attached his arms. Three more buffeted his body, hitting with enough force to crack his ribs.

Mark thrashed and splashed, the shallow water barely deep enough keep him submerged. Chlöe's frantic screams echoed in his ears, but try as he might, Mark could not escape. The onslaught knocked the breath from his body. Water poured down his throat and into his lungs. Coughing and spluttering, Mark drowned, the taste of his own blood tainting the water.

When the thrashings finally ceased, Chlöe stared at the still form in the water, willing him to move, but he didn't. Mark was dead, and she was alone.

The tide chased her down. Sand that had been dry when Chlöe heaved her body from the water grew damp. The ocean was hungry, and it was coming for her.

Chlöe focused on the tideline further up the beach. She recalled Maria saying that at certain times of the year, the entire bay would be filled with water.

Inching her way up the beach, her body weak from the loss of blood, and the state of shock that flirted with her consciousness, Chlöe cried.

The water gained on her. Each lunge she made moved her less and less. The water reached her feet, and then her knees. The fish were waiting for her, their bodies squirming back and forth in the shallows.

Tired, her energy spent, the adrenaline that had coursed through her body long since depleted, Chlöe admitted defeat. Laying back in the sand, Chlöe cried. Gazing at the cloudless blue sky, she lost herself in its expanse. Flinching as the tide crept under her body. It was almost time. She hoped it wouldn't hurt.

The first nibble at her remaining foot proved her wrong.

CHAPTER 8

Troy fidgeted nervously. He did not want to look desperate. He had been sitting on the terrace for close to an hour, waiting for Melissa to arrive. He waited because he had nothing else to do, his time being free of all other commitments and obligations, yet, he did not want to appear over eager.

"I'm so sorry," Melissa began, looking at the ground as she emerged from her holiday home.

"It's fine, you're right on time. We have all day." Troy smiled at her.

"No, it's not that. It's ... well, the scuba guy called and said he would be available for the lesson today. So I need to ..." Melissa paused. Looking at him, her face reddened with spreading embarrassment.

"You need to cancel our snorkelling adventure," Troy said, picking up from where she left off.

"Yes, and I am really sorry. I hope it doesn't mess up your plans," Melissa added, shifting from one foot to another.

She smiled, and Troy realized he had not seen anything cuter in all his days.

"That's alright, we can always go tomorrow ... if you still want to, that is." Troy found himself oddly nervous as he made the proposition.

"I'd like that, shall we say the same time?"

"That sounds perfect to me."

"Great, but I have to run now. See you, bye." Melissa turned and hurried away, and Troy returned to his spot on the terrace.

Troy sat for a few moments, debating how to spend his day, and ultimately sliding into the pool, cooling himself off while he made up his mind.

Raul met Melissa by the pool, apologizing for the repeated change of plans, assuring her that under normal circumstances he was much more reliable with regards his appointments and time keeping.

Melissa accepted his apology, and did not push for anything more. Her journalist's nose led her to believe there was more to it. Something in Raul's voice seemed different to the first time she met him. She forced it away, however, reminding herself that she was on a holiday.

"So, are you ready to explore a new world?" he asked with a smile. His demeanour was much more relaxed, much more like that first impression on the beach.

"Yes, I am. I've always wanted to go diving." Melissa did not want to admit that, now she was actually having a lesson, a certain degree of fear had crept into her mind.

"Great, then let's get started. I don't want to take up all of your time." Raul turned and handed Melissa a wetsuit and flippers. "These will be enough for now."

After testing her abilities as a swimmer, and forcing her through several straightforward underwater drills, Raul grabbed the oxygen tanks and help Melissa into the gear. It was heavier than she expected, but once they dropped into the pool, everything changed.

Melissa took to the diving like a natural, impressing Raul with her abilities. He gave Melissa the freedom to explore the pool and get used to the way her body responded in the water.

The tremor came as a surprise. Short, but powerful. Melissa jumped underwater, the respirator mouthpiece flew from her gasping mouth. Before she could stop herself, Melissa took a deep breath, forgetting she was underwater. She coughed and choked, kicking her way to the surface of the pool relieved when Raul reached down and helped her out of the water.

"That felt like an earthquake," she panted, as she regained control of her body.

"It was. Out to sea. They occur quite frequently in these parts, but I will admit, they are not normally so strong that we feel them on land," Raul answered.

His words were soothing, and had Melissa been any other person, she would have accepted the answer and walked away, eager to see the back of the pool, all ideas of learning to dive shaken from her mind. Melissa, however, was not like other people. She sensed something in Raul, a story. Standing her ground, Melissa slid out of holiday mode and into the realm she felt most comfortable.

"How often do you have earthquakes like that?" she asked,

"Out at sea?"

"Yes."

"It's hard to tell. I don't monitor them. But sometimes, when you are out on the water, you can feel something. They are not big events, probably barely register on any scale." Raul held Melissa's gaze, playing her at the game she loved.

"But you said you don't often feel them on land. What does that mean? This one must have been strong enough to register, right?" Melissa pushed, knowing she had Raul on a very thin line.

"Let me guess, you are a reporter, out in the real world?" Raul's sudden change of conversational tack caught Melissa by surprise.

"I am, yes, how could you tell?" Melissa asked.

"I know that look. That voice. You see, my ex-wife was a reporter. Got her into all sorts of trouble while we were together."

"Then you know, I know, you know something," Melissa pushed, hoping she had not lost Raul's attention.

"I really do not. I'm sorry. Like I said, not often do you have a tremor that reaches the land, but trust me, the resort staff will warn you if there is anything to worry about. For now, I would suggest you just relax and enjoy your holiday. Nothing is going on here, and there is no reason to panic." Raul turned his attention back to the pool and tidying away the scuba gear.

"What about the rest of my lessons?" Melissa asked.

"Come and see me tomorrow, I am sure we can arrange something. I want to keep you in the pool for now, maybe one more lesson and then we can hit the beach." Raul didn't turn around as he spoke, and Melissa convinced herself he was covering for something. Maybe he didn't know what was going on, but the events concerned him more than he let on.

Melissa left and as she walked back through the resort she looked around. Everybody was continuing on their way as if nothing had happened. Oblivious in the extreme to the events going on around them.

She argued with herself as she walked. A silent diatribe. *You take everything too seriously. You should relax. It was nothing. Raul said it. Nobody else is panicking. Just let it go. Have a drink, and maybe you will run into Troy. He's cute.*

Melissa broke out of her trance just before she walked into the man that stood on the path before her.

She looked up and gasped when she saw Troy standing inches away from her, smiling, glistening with sweat, a towel around his neck.

"Oh, hi, sorry … I um … I just, I was miles away," she stammered feeling the blush spreading.

Melissa always wondered why she could chase down a lead without fear, but talking to someone on a social level, left her a stuttering fool.

"I saw that. How did your scuba lesson go?" Troy smiled at her and Melissa's legs swooned a little.

Get a hold of yourself, woman. "Oh, good. I mean, well, other than the earthquake." If she held any hope of talking to Troy without sounding like a stupid schoolgirl, she needed to use a subject matter she could translate to the serious side of her subconscious.

"Earthquake? What are you talking about?" Troy looked puzzled.

"You didn't feel it?"

"No, but I was in the gym. I kind of zone out then." He pointed to the right, indicating the exact location. He laughed nervously, and lowered his arm. "I wouldn't worry about that quake. If anything serious happened, then the resort would warn us."

"Oh, I'm sure of it. But, well … it just feels a little off," Melissa said, slumping her shoulders. Troy was right, she was overreacting, but at the same time, she could not shake the strange feeling of unease pulling at the edges of her mind.

"What you need is something to take your mind off of things. How about I grab a quick shower and then we can head for some lunch?"

"That would be nice, but I have to collect my daughter from that kids' place. I promised her we would hang out by the water slides this afternoon." Melissa lowered her head as she spoke. She did not like rejecting Troy's advances.

"That's all good. We are still on for tomorrow though, right?" He turned to walk away.

"For snorkelling, yes. It's a date," Melissa said with a cough, hoping the sound would somehow mask what she had said.

Troy stopped in his stride and turned to look at her. Melissa's cheeks burned with flush, and said a silent prayer to have the ground open up and swallow her.

Try smiled and gave her a wink. "Sounds good to me," he said, and was gone, disappearing into a crowd of people moving from the beach to the restaurant.

Melissa searched for any sign of Troy, but couldn't see him on any of the three pathways in the immediate vicinity. She gave a sigh and walked away, still embarrassed by what she said, but at the same time, she found herself excited by the way he had reacted.

Rachel sat waiting for her mother in the large playground. A huge smile plastered onto her face. She proudly showed off the tie-dye T-shirt that she had made during the morning.

"That's very pretty," Melissa said, smiling and hugging her daughter.

"Thanks, dying stuff is great fun, and super easy. Can we try it when we get back home?" She bounced as they walked, her excitement spilling over into her words, which came at a rush.

"Oh, I'm sure we can. Good grief, you are already so brown." Melissa stared at her daughter's deeply tanned arms. "It's only been a day. You are just like your father with that." Melissa stopped walking and caught her words.

"What's wrong?" Rachel asked.

"Nothing, honey. I was just thinking about how much you look like your dad." Melissa tried to control the tremble that always crept into her voice when she thought about her ex-husband. Her confusing feelings for the sexy man in the chalet next to them made for an interesting component.

"Do you know where Daddy is?" Rachel asked, innocent and oblivious to the hard truths of the world.

"No, honey, I don't. Not right now." Melissa shook away the emotions. "Come on, I am in the mood for some pizza. I will race you to the top of the dragonfly slide, winner chooses the toppings."

The distraction worked for both of them. They spent the afternoon careening through the twists and turns of the parks multiple water slides. Going down face first, feet first, on their bellies, and on their backs. For the first time in a long time, Melissa let go of the world. It was hard to tell who enjoyed the day more, mother or daughter.

They sat in the restaurant for a long time, eating way too much pizza and salad. Melissa fell for a lovely bottle of red wine, while Rachel moved from coke to water midway through the meal.

Rachel could hardly keep her eyes open by the time they returned to their chalet that evening. Melissa felt great, carrying more than a little buzz from the wine. Her stomach did a somersault when she moved into their cul-de-sac of chalets to find Troy sitting outside, nursing a beer from the nearby bar.

"Why don't you go inside and head straight to bed? You can shower in the morning," Melissa said.

"You like him, don't you, Mummy?" Rachel whispered,

"What?"

"The man next door. You like him. He is very nice. I like him."

"Rachel Stone, you do not get to talk to your mother like that." Melissa tried to sound stern, but both she and Rachel recognized a bluff when they heard one. Besides, Rachel was not wrong.

Melissa did not want to put a label on her feelings for Troy. The attraction spoke for itself, no doubt about it, and the lust … that was a given. Melissa could not act on those urges, however. Not with her daughter around.

"Good night, Mummy." Rachel moved onto her tiptoes, stretching to give her mother a kiss on the cheek.

She disappeared inside and Melissa fell into the chair.

"Long day?" Troy asked after a few moments.

"Long day," Melissa answered. "Good day, but a long day."

Sitting there, Melissa giggled. She didn't know why, it just happened. Turning at the sound of movement, she gasped. Troy stood leaning on the small wall that separate their terraces.

"Fancy a drink?" he asked, raising his now empty glass.

"I could go for a beer," she answered quickly, too quickly for her own good.

"Cool, I'll be right back." Troy hurried away, returning a few moments later with two beers.

"Want to join me?" Melissa asked.

"Thank you." Troy slid into the second chair.

They sat together and talked until long after the sun went down. They drank several beers, and by the end of it, Melissa left buzzed for dust and was officially drunk.

"I think we had better call it a night," Troy said when Melissa went to stand and pretty much fell straight over to her left.

"You're very strong," Melissa giggled, as Troy scooped her into his arms.

"Well, I do work out." Troy smiled.

He carried Melissa into her chalet and up the stairs. The layout was identical to that of his own holiday home, and so he figured out which room Melissa used as her own.

As he placed her on the bed, she woke. Wrapping her arms around his neck, she pulled Troy close to her and kissed him.

Troy moved away, but Melissa pulled him back again. Her lips found his, her tongue traced his. She moaned and pulled Troy closer still.

"Not like this," he said, moving away gently.

"It's okay," she slurred.

"It's all good, but not tonight, not like this." Troy stood up from the bed, Melissa already falling asleep.

"Thank you," she said, as he walked out of the room.

"Any time. Get some sleep, we have a date tomorrow after all." Troy turned the light off and headed back to his own place.

CHAPTER 9

The following morning, Troy sat waiting for Melissa, but as he assumed, she did not come down. She had a lot to sleep off. Troy sipped his coffee when he heard movement from the house next door. Rachel appeared in the doorway; wandering out to the terrace, she sat down and looked in his direction.

"Good morning," Troy said.

"Hi."

"I think your mum is going to have a late morning." He looked at the girl, who placed a thick book on the table. Troy couldn't catch the full name, but saw the word Kaiju on the spine.

"That's okay," Rachel answered.

"Well, I'm going to go down for some breakfast. Want to join me?" Troy offered. "We can leave your mum a note."

"Um… okay, I guess." Rachel eyed Troy suspiciously. "My mum likes you, you know."

"I kind of had that impression too," Troy said, nodding.

"You had better not hurt her." Rachel's eyes burned fiercely for a moment, before returning to their hazel shade.

"I wouldn't dream of it. Scout's honour." Troy raised his hand.

"What does that mean?"

"Never mind. I'm old."

Rachel scribbled a note for her mother, and ran back out to Troy. In spite of all the pizza the night before, Rachel was starving, and pretty sure Troy would let her eat whatever she wanted for breakfast. Including cake.

She could not have been more wrong.

***

By the time they returned to the chalet, Melissa had stumbled from her bed and out into the open air, a large coffee in a

Styrofoam cup clenched in both hands. She jumped when Rachel called her name, turning a deep beetroot when her eyes met Troy's.

"Thanks for taking her to breakfast," she said, averting her eyes to look at her daughter.

"Oh, it was my pleasure. She's quite the character," Troy spoke.

"Mum, he made me eat fruit, and bran flakes." Rachel pouted, protesting to her mother, the same way she had protested to Troy's insistence that she eat a healthy breakfast before starting in on the bacon and eggs.

"Did he now?" Melissa smiled, looking at Troy and holding her composure as she did.

"I did, she told me you normally just let her eat cake." Troy winked at Melissa.

"Did she now?" Melissa's eyes flared in the same way her daughter's did.

"Mum ... bran flakes." Rachel crossed her arms and pouted.

"I told her it wasn't a good idea. So yeah, we made a deal bran flakes first and then cake."

"You didn't." Melissa turned her flaring gaze towards Troy.

"She insisted." Troy pointed at Rachel.

"Hey, at least I ate them. You just ate bacon." Rachel looked accusingly at Troy.

"No, I also had some white bread and ketchup. Tomato's a fruit you know." Troy smiled and gave Rachel a gentle shove.

She giggled and moved towards the house. "I need to shower before the Kids' Klub. Later, Troy." She waved, disappearing inside the chalet.

"Nice kid," Troy said, sitting down at the table.

"I'm sorry about last night," Melissa blurted it out.

"It's fine," Troy answered, his soft spoken words and gentle attitude a distinct comfort. Yet Rachel's abject horror at her actions would not be diluted by kind words.

"Maybe so, but still. That ... that isn't me. I never do that. I barely drink." Stammering again, Rachel needed to convince him, and herself, of the truth.

"You're on holiday, acting out of character is allowed." Troy reached over and took her hand in his. "Besides, you are cute when you blush."

"I like you, I mean, I don't know you, but I'm attracted to you, and I don't want you to think it is just because I was drunk, or that I do it all the time."

"I don't. I'll tell you what. Why don't we both change, bring the sprog to her club, and we can go snorkelling? You can show me the real you. A date is a date after all." Troy stood up, leaned over and kissed Melissa on the cheek.

She said nothing, the blush on her cheeks darkening even further.

They walked to the beach, on the southern area of the island, where a large, manmade reef stood just off the shore. Built by the resort, they guaranteed a great range of species and sightings each dive.

"Have you done this before?" Troy asked.

"A long time ago, but it is fairly straight forward, if I remember rightly." Melissa smiled.

"That it is." They were decked out in rental flippers, diving masks, and snorkels.

Troy elected to wear a pair of colourful swim shorts that looked like Bermudan boxing trunks. Melissa could not help but steal glances of his muscular physique. His solid, flat abs and the round shoulders. A series of large bruises covered his ribs. They looked painful, but she didn't dare ask.

"They are from my last fight. I took a few hard knees in the first round," Troy answered, reading her mind.

"How did you know ... wait a second, were you checking me out?" Melissa asked

"What ... um, no, I just figured, you had seen the bruises and ... yeah." The blush burned his cheeks.

"You were, you were checking me out in my bikini," Melissa laughed.

Troy didn't answer. He took a big step and pushed himself out into the sea. The soothing water cooled his burning flesh. The reef was some way ahead of them, but already small fish swam about, inspecting the newest stranger to invade their habitat.

Troy did not believe that fish could not be trained, and from what he had read, their memories were nothing to write home about, as they neared the reef, the fish did not flee as he swam to them.

He saw a shadow glide alongside him. Turning his head, he watched Melissa swim, her body moving through the water gracefully, her slender legs kicking her ahead of Troy. She turned around in the water, and he knew she was showing off, giving him the time to check out the rest of her.

They came to the surface in an embrace, their bodies pressing against one another, the water reaching the top of Melissa's breasts.

They had the reef pretty much to themselves, most people choosing to lounge at the center of the resort, but enough people flittered around to rule out any acts of lust-driven stupidity. They kissed. A real kiss this time. Their lips met and the world fell away around them.

"We should probably check out the reef, while we are here," Melissa spoke between embraces.

"You're right, we really should," Troy said with a smile.

Reluctantly, they parted and allowed the ocean to temper the fire that had been lit within them both.

The reef was beautiful; just over half a mile long and populated by every sort of fish they could imagine, most of which neither could name. Epilate sharks walked over the ocean floor, darting around the reef bed. Schools of small fish swam to and fro around them; darting around the coral sections without a care in the world. Troy even spotted a few clownfish nestled around the large patch of anemone.

They did not swim the whole length of the reef, but swam back and forth over the same section for quite some time. The reef had a peaceful and romantic quality. The warm sun on their backs, the pull of the tide and the sway of the ocean.

They would come up to the surface every now and then, stealing a kiss from one another.

"It's stunning out here," Melissa said as they sat down in the shallow water. She lay back, the water not deep enough to fully submerge her.

"It is, and the reef isn't too shabby either," Troy said.

"Oh no, nope, sorry, that is too cheesy. You are going to have to try again." Melissa sat up and splashed him with water.

She laughed, and gave a little scream when Troy returned fire.

Lost in laughter and moderate flirting, both were oblivious to the first tremor which came rumbling through the sea floor. While gentler than the one the previous day, it made up for the initial weakness in rumble that followed a few moments later.

The sea became choppy. The change coming in from behind the reef. The water broke as the tide surged over the structure, petering out before it made land.

The pull of the ocean was immense though, and both jumped to their feet to avoid being pulled away.

"What the heck?" Troy looked around for any signs of panic.

"Another earthquake. Something is going on out here. I'm sure of it," Melissa said.

"Help me," a voice called out.

Troy turned, and reacted before Melissa had the chance to spot the troubled swimmer. Troy disappeared into the water, swimming towards the reef, not surfacing until he reached the structure. Only then did Melissa see the man hailing them. Trapped on the other side of the reef, the unlucky swimmer found themselves caught by the undercurrent, which pulled them out to sea.

Around them, people began to scream. The second tremor hit and shook the ground they stood on, causing panic to settle. People ran from the water, fleeing the beach. Many continued to run, disappearing into the island in an attempt to outrun the shuddering ground.

The tremor stopped and the ocean calmed. The panic remained, with the beach all but empty. An alarm echoed down from the resort, and for the first time, Melissa began to panic. She thought of Rachel, and turned to run. She looked back at the reef, where Troy was busy hauling a struggling figure back to the beach.

Melissa froze and ran back into the water to help Troy. Rachel was safe, in good hands with the resort staff around her. The tremor ended and did not appear to have caused any damage.

Rachel remembered reading somewhere, in some pamphlet or another, about an alarm on the beach. It sounded automatically when people needed to get out of the water.

"Here, let me help." Melissa reached out and took hold of the man's legs.

The man was still half submerged in the water, his resistance weakening with every heaved effort Troy made, the water around them turning red with blood. The deep, jagged wound in the man's calf supplied the crimson-coloured dye.

"Help me pull him out of the water," Troy said, taking most of the man's weight as they lifted the body into the air.

"What happened to him?"

"Best I can tell is he got caught on the coral. It's deep, he needs medical attention," Troy said.

They rested the man on the shore, using a discarded towel to hold his bleeding calf out of the sand. Shaking uncontrollably, he soon passed out, and his agonized screams fell still.

"We can't move him alone. I need you to run and get some help. I'll stay with him. Send anybody you can, and then check on your little girl. Make sure she is safe." Troy said, taking charge.

"Thank you," Melissa said.

She rose and sprinted down the beach, disappearing into the trees of the resort and out of sight.

Troy waited by the man, using the elastic strapping of his face mask to create a crude tourniquet, which he applied to the man's leg. Alone, Troy studied the wound. Something did not sit easy with him. He had seen something out by the reef. Only a fleeting glance, whatever it was disappeared into the murky water. The disturbed seabed reduced visibility, and Troy had been busy with other efforts at the time.

***

"Do you have any idea what those things are?" Melissa asked as they sat eating dinner.

Rachel sat with them in the Italian-themed eatery. After the second quake, the resort continued to function as normal, although some of the taller water slides had closed for a few hours, out of precaution.

"I am not sure. I definitely saw something, but it could have been one of the reef sharks, disturbed by the quake, it's just … well…" Troy stopped talking and looking towards Rachel.

"Oh, it's fine, she's not listening to us. Are you, honey?" Melissa said to her oblivious child.

Troy laughed. "That wound on his leg, it looked like a bite more than anything else."

"A bite?"

"Yeah, and something pretty big would be needed to do damage like that." Troy pushed his pasta around the plate as he spoke.

"You mean like a shark?" Melissa asked, her reporter's brain starting to run.

"I don't know. I mean, maybe, but … what about those earthquakes? They are happening a lot. It's four in a few days, right?" Troy stared at Melissa. His mind was busy trying to find sense in the swirling myriad of thoughts bouncing around inside his skull.

"Yes, at least that many. When did they start? My scuba instructor said they were not uncommon, but I think he was holding back, hiding something," Melissa said, sensing that Troy's mind worked in a similar fashion to her own.

"This resort is manmade, right? What if these quakes are not earthquakes exactly, but the foundations of the island?" The image in Troy's head began to clear as he voiced the words.

"You mean this place could be falling apart?" Melissa smelled the story potential.

'Well, maybe, or it is just settling. I mean, this place is new, right? I mean, you would assume they would let it settle before they opened, but you never know anymore. People are more interested in opening, and turning a few extra bucks. In any case, I'd love to go back out to the reef again, both to take a look around, and to finish our date." Troy winked, eager to change the topic of conversation. More than anything, to give his mind time to settle.

He grabbed some garlic bread and dipped it in the sauce on his plate.

***

"There's something down there, just beyond the reef. Maybe thirty or forty yards. Just as the coast drops away and it starts getting deep," Troy said as he waded out of the water.

Melissa sat in the sand, waiting for him; Rachel sat beside her, digging a hole with her hands. The Kids' Klub did not operate on a Thursday, and so she tagged along with her mother and Troy. She enjoyed playing in the water, practicing how to use the snorkel and flippers, listening to Troy's instructions as if they were gospel.

"What do you think it is?" Melissa asked, looking up at Troy, shielding her eyes from the sun.

"I don't know. It looks like a crack in the floor. Some sort of trench." Troy sat down in the shallows and closed his eyes, enjoying the sun's warmth on his skin.

"It must have been the earthquakes," Melissa said, feeling a strange sense of vindication in her reporter's intuition.

"Either that or it is an existing trench that people overlooked," Troy offered as a counterpoint.

"Maybe both. Maybe the ground was unstable, but they built on it anyway. That might have triggered the quakes, creating the chasm?" Melissa pondered aloud.

"Could be. I'm going to head out and take a close look at it. Want to tag along?" he asked Melissa.

"Sure. Hey, Rachel, we are going up to the reef. I want you to stay here, okay? I will be back in ten minutes," Melissa called out to her child.

"Okay, Mum."

Troy took the lead, swimming out ahead. He reached the reef and signalled for Melissa to wait. He disappeared beneath the surface, coming up a few moments later to give the all clear signal.

"Care to explain?" Melissa smiled

"Checking for sharks," Troy answered.

"Aw, my hero." Melissa splashed water in Troy's face.

"The seabed slopes away sharply about thirty or so yards out. That was where I thought I saw something … you don't think we are being stupid, do you?" Troy's face scrunched up in self-doubt.

"I think something is going on, and it can't hurt to investigate," Melissa answered. She cast a glance back towards the beach where Rachel waited, patiently playing in the water.

Troy swam over the reef and gasped when the water temperature suddenly changed, telling him he was in the right spot, above the trench. He took several deep breaths, breathing faster and faster before taking a final large deep gulp of air and diving below the surface.

The water was clear, the disruption caused by the quake long-since settled. Troy spotted the trench without needing to dive down to the bottom. The long crack moved over the seabed like a jagged lightning bolt. It moved along the same axis as the reef and the rest of the island.

Troy pulled himself deeper, his vision caught by something along the crack. A stream of bubbles came from within the gash. As Troy moved further away from the reef, the full magnitude of the crack came into view. It stretched away into the distance, widening to a point approximately three meters across at its peak.

Troy returned to the surface and took a deep breath. He disappeared immediately again, as movement beneath his feet pulled his attention. A large brown fish passed beneath him. It was at least twenty-four inches in length, cylindrical at the head tapering down to the tail.

It swam below Troy, who could not get a good look at the creature. When it turned, he caught sight of the teeth. There was very little else to be seen, for they appeared to consume its entire head. Large curved teeth that appeared almost translucent in the water. Too large for the jaws, they extended both above and below, shielding the head like a cage.

The creature seemed to stop in the water, its body angled so that it stared at Troy. The large brown eyes bulged behind the mesh of teeth. Troy froze. The fish moved. It charged at Troy, the jaws opening as it closed the distance. Everything happened in an instant. Troy kicked with his legs, pulled with his arms and avoided the attack. He tucked and rolled underwater, throwing out a hand to grab hold of the fish.

He clenched his fist and pulled, but the creature was too strong. The fish spun around, the body folding close to double on itself. The jaws snapped again, Troy just able to avoid being bitten. He swiped again, trying to throw a jab at the thing's head. The fish turned away, its body slamming into Troy with enough force to push the remaining air from his lungs.

Kicking frantically, Troy headed for the surface. He burst from the water with the grace of a breaching whale. He splashed and crashed, trying to swim away while at the same time allowing the oxygen to re-enter his body.

In that moment, Troy's world shrank to two things: himself, and the fish. The rest fell away, no longer holding any meaning. The world slowed down, the fight began. Troy kicked with his legs, and pulled with his arms. The resistance of the water as he powered his way to the shore, took on a new meaning, a heightened sensation of the climb, of movement and motion. The fish was still nearby, he knew it, even if he could no longer see the creature, due to the water bubbling around him as a result of his rapid strokes.

Behind him, something splashed in the water. Troy reacted, snatching his feet towards him, using his upper body strength to pull himself beneath the water. His mask had come loose in the struggle. Water filled it, blurring his vision. He could make out the reef beneath him. He kicked down to the seabed, pulling himself along the reef, jagged sections of coral cutting into his flesh like a surgeon's scalpel.

Troy winced against the pain. The water clouded with blood. Movement caught his eye. Troy pushed himself upwards, his chest burning from exertion and oxygen starvation. The change in his momentum took up away from the fish, which crashed into the rock-based portion of the reef.

Troy broke the surface and swam back to shore, running from the moment his feet could reach the seabed.

"Get out, get out of the water," he waved his arms and shouted at Melissa, who scooped Rachel into her arms and ran out of the water.

Troy ran, tripped, and fell into the shallows. He pushed himself to his feet and ran onto the shore. He heard Melissa scream, but would not allow himself to turn around. He ran from the surf and collapsed onto his hands and knees on the beach.

Unable to moved, breathing heavily, Troy remained on all fours for some time. The ache in his hands began to register in his brain and brought Troy back down into reality.

He turned and sat on the beach. Melissa moved beside him. In the distance, further back Rachel sat quietly, her knees drawn up to her chest. She had screamed herself hoarse as Troy fought his way back to the beach.

"What was that thing?" Melissa asked

Troy looked at her. Without offering a response, he wrapped his arms around her and pulled her close.

"It leaped out of the water when you fell. It looked horrid. I've never seen anything like it before," Melissa spoke, separating from Troy so she could take a look at his bleeding hands. "Oh my God. Somebody needs to take a look at these."

"It came from the trench. That crack goes on for a long way and gets really wide. Whatever attacked me came from within it." Troy moved his gaze from Melissa to the ocean and back again. A constant loop, as if afraid to take his gaze away from either one for too long.

"You mean it swam through it, like a slip road?" Melissa asked, not following the trail of thought. How could she?

"No, this thing was big. It doesn't belong here. I refuse to believe they would have continued building the reef out here if they knew that thing lived in the waters. It came from in the trench, I am sure of it. When the quake happened, this thing woke up." Troy shuddered at the thought.

"You mean like a ... like a ... sea monster?" Melissa said full of seriousness, painfully aware of how ludicrous it sounded.

"I don't know, but whatever it is, it doesn't belong in our world. We need to warn people. If that's not the only one..." Troy stopped talking and stared into Melissa's eyes. Relief swept through him when she nodded her head, removing the need for him to further explain himself.

Melissa used a clean shirt from her bag to wrap Troy's hands. The wounds bled profusely, but did not appear to be too deep. Together, the three of them hurried back to the resort.

CHAPTER 10

The resort was a happy and joyous place; the hoots and hollers of the guests by the pool, the laughter and almost musical clink of cutlery that drifted out of the restaurants. All a stark and crazy contrast to the frantic events of the beach. Even Rachel laughed at it.

"It's like they don't even know," she said, pointing out the change in atmosphere with the ease only a child can truly muster.

"They don't," Melissa said to her daughter.

Troy was quiet. His hands hurt from the cuts, and his head ached from tumultuous thoughts about his championship fight. As trivial as it was given the situation on the resort, he had fought so hard to reach the number one spot again. The notion that it could once again be so easily ripped away from him weighed heavily on his mind.

"Where are we going?" Rachel asked. "We need to tell people. They need to stay away from the water."

"Yes, they do, sweetie. We are going to the resort manager. We are going to tell him what we saw. We can't make him do anything, though," Melissa said, speaking to her daughter like a friend.

"What about Troy? His hands are hurt," Rachel asked, squeezing between the two adults to give Troy's arm a hug.

"Troy is going to go to the doctors in the main hotel. They will put him back together, and then we will take care of the fish problem," Melissa said, allaying her daughter's concerns.

"We need to visit the manager first," Troy protested as Melissa, with the help of Rachel, guided his stubborn frame towards the medical rooms.

"Don't worry. I will go talk to him. You just need to get stitched back together. You're a fighter, you need your hands in good working order." He smiled, and thought his chest might explode.

"You really do care about me." He smiled.

"That and I am pretty sure my ex-husband will have a pretty big chunk of change on the champ, so I want you in the ring ready to knock him out." She returned the smile as she spoke.

"Ouch, you parted that badly?" Troy winced as the nurse, who had been moving silently around them, undid the makeshift wrapping on his hands.

"Oh no, not at all. We parted well enough. It just wasn't meant to be. We were young, in love. We had it all, but sometimes things just don't work out," Melissa spoke about it with ease, telling Troy she was not lying to spare him any long-winded rants.

"Is he around much?" Troy asked phishing, but he could fall back on the theory of distraction from the stitches if Melissa called him on it.

"No, not much. He calls when he can, but he is not around very often. That's one of the things that drove us apart." Melissa looked at the floor.

Troy did not need to be a mind-reader to know that the subject needed to be changed. He did not want to upset Melissa. Something was developing between them, and he wanted to explore it.

"You had better go and find the manager. Try to convince him to keep people out of the water. Call somebody down to investigate." Troy winced a little as the first needle pierced his skin.

"Wish me luck," Melissa said. She leaned in and planted a kiss on Troy's cheek.

"Good luck," Troy said as she walked away.

His view of her departure was blocked by the nurse, whose face filled his field of vision. She glared at him with the judgemental gaze of an old-school teacher staring at the naughty kid in class.

"Lie back," she said, her bedside manner cold and clinical.

Melissa left Troy to his sutures, and headed over to the main hotel area. She strode in and directed Rachel towards a chair in the lobby. "Don't move until I come back, alright?" she ordered.

"Okay," Rachel said, falling into the chair. The events from the beach did not seem to be affecting her too badly.

"Excuse me, I want to talk to the manager," Melissa whispered to the young woman behind the desk.

"I'm sorry, ma'am. Can I be of help?" she asked.

Melissa looked at the woman, studying her. The beautiful face and long black hair. The slender frame and perfectly perky breasts that pushed against her shirt at just the right angle to make more women jealous.

"No, you really can't. I have to speak with the manager," Melissa insisted.

"Ma'am, I am afraid that is not possible," the woman behind the counter insisted. Her prim and proper demeanour slipping just enough to let her attitude to shine through.

"Listen, I don't give a crap. You will take me through to the director now, or I will raise merry Hell telling everybody about the cockroach problem in the kitchen," Melissa spoke with a growl, her voice calm in that threatening way.

The young woman behind the desk stammered, caught by surprise and left in with no false impression that the threat was anything other than genuine.

"I will check if he is available," she stuttered.

"Take me to him," Melissa demanded, raising her voice just enough to generate a few inquisitive looks from the people checking in further down the reception area.

"Yes, of course, ma'am," the young woman answered.

She led Melissa through the back area of the hotel, up two flights of stairs to the manager's office.

It was a large room with an expansive view of the ocean. A single, large window formed the far wall. It filled the office with light and a magnificent view of the ocean. Melissa had been in enough meeting rooms over the years to know the power a nice view had over visitors.

"Mr. Guerrero, I have a guest here who wants to talk to you," the receptionist spoke in English, before dropping into Spanish, no doubt relaying the threats she had received and the crazy nature of the woman she had brought up. As she unburdened herself, passing the problem over to her boss, the worry left her face.

Melissa felt a pang of guilt, at the thought that the woman could lose her job or be punished for bringing her to the office. She forced it away, knowing her actions were in the interest of safety. People on the resort were in danger, and that trumped a job; besides, if everybody died, the entire resort would be closed, and the women would be in the same predicament, only with a large therapy requirement added to her list of worries.

The manager replied to the woman in Spanish, and she left the room looking relieved. She did save a short, sharp scowl for Melissa, glaring at her as she passed. Melissa didn't blame her.

"I understand you wanted to speak to me, Miss —"

"Stone, Melissa Stone. Thank you for seeing me. There is a huge problem in the water, and you need to close the beaches," Melissa blurted it out, finding the gentle approach redundant when introducing a theory as crazy as hers.

"Alright, I understand. What reasoning do you have for this drastic course of action?" The manager, Hugo Guerrero, stared at Melissa, his eyes narrowing into a squint. He was a short, stocky man with a thick moustache that hid his upper lip completely.

"There is a monster in the water. Those earthquakes from the yesterday and the day before, they opened up a large fissure in the ground. Something came out of it, something big. People are going to end up hurt, or worse. Like that man on the reef yesterday." Melissa stopped herself, catching her anger, as she tried to explain as much as she could, without sounding any madder than she already did.

"Aha, I see. Yes, I heard about the accident yesterday. I can assure you, those injuries were nothing more than the result of a man ignoring the rules and getting too close to the reef itself. Sea monsters do not exist, Miss Stone." The man remained seating behind his desk, his hands folded over one another, the elbows resting on the arms of his chair.

"You don't believe me, do you?" Melissa shot back at him.

"I think you were on the beach yesterday, maybe even in the water. You got a fright. It is hot, the sun is strong. Not forgetting the quakes you mentioned are bound to put you on edge," Hugo began, but Melissa charged at him like an enraged bull.

"How dare you. I am coming to you to warn you that people are going to get hurt if you do not listen to me." Melissa knew her words sounded like a threat, but it did not make them any less true. "There is something out there, maybe multiple somethings. You need to take this seriously, or people are going to die."

"Young lady, I do not appreciate you coming in here threatening me. I do not care what you think is going to happen. This resort is state of the art in every possible way. We have perimeter nets that will keep out everything that we do not want getting in. We have sensors positioned everywhere. I appreciate you raising a concern, but such issues can be handled by my staff. Now please, relax and enjoy your stay with us. Maybe try a cocktail or two in our Blue Oyster beach bar. Trust me, they are very good." Hugo sat back in his chair and stared at Melissa, making it abundantly clear he did not intend to spend any more time discussing the issue.

"You are a prick. When things go to shit, don't say I didn't warn you. If you gave a damn, you would get up, and go check on the man from yesterday. Then you would know, that injury wasn't from the coral. Maybe even send a few people out into the water, and check out the big crack that runs the far side of the reef. Hell, at least check with some others," Melissa roared, shouting as her temper flared.

Hugo jumped to his feet, the moustache billowing beneath his nose as he snarled. "How dare you. Get out of this office right now, and if I catch you so much as near the lobby, or hear you threatening anybody else, then I will see to it that you are removed from this resort. Now good day to you." Hugo's raised voice was filled with anger, but it paled in comparison to the fury bubbling in Melissa's gut. She did not flinch at his words, however, understanding when to stop flogging the donkey.

"I'll leave, but you will be sorry. You will wish you had listened to me," Melissa spat, turned on her heels, and stormed from the office. She slammed the door as she left, an act of petulant good measure, but she felt better for it.

Melissa glared at the woman behind the desk as she stormed out of the hotel. Rachel heard her mother coming and met her by the door.

"What did he say?" Rachel asked as she hurried to keep up with her mother.

"He was a jerk," Melissa said as they walked out into the sun.

Rachel giggled, but for the rest she said nothing.

Troy made it back to the chalet first and sat waiting for them. The medical staff managed to clean and suture his hands, before binding them in thick layers of bandages.

Melissa looked at him and made a mocking sad face. "Those look pretty," she said, and beside her, Rachel giggled.

"Feels like I'm getting taped up for a fight." Troy smiled, making fists and taking up a stance.

"Does it hurt?" Rachel asked.

"No, it stings a little, but I'll survive," he answered her, before turning his focus to Melissa. "How did it go?"

"The guy is an ass. He refused to listen, and got mad, he even claimed I threatened him." Melissa didn't want to relive the conversation. Sure, hindsight suggested better ways of handling the situation, but dwelling on them would not change a thing. The man was a twat.

"What do we do now?" Troy asked.

"What can we do? Wait, I guess. I mean, whatever is out there is only in the water. The rest of the park is fine. I mean … I don't know. I'm not saying we should just get back to holidaying and leave it, but maybe a distraction would be good. You know. We can't change anything if they don't want to listen." Melissa fell into the chair beside Troy.

"Well, I am hungry. So why don't we all go grab some food?" Troy offered.

"Yeah can we go eat, Mum? I'm starving," Rachel spoke up.

***

Troy woke the next morning, and for a moment, had no idea in whose bed he lay. His hands itched, and when he saw the thick wrapping, his mind went blank. Wrapping normally meant a fight, but he remembered his last fight. Then things came back to him. He sat up in bed. With the sun streaming through the window, Troy stretched. He could not recall waking up so rested in a long time.

"Morning," Melissa spoke, sitting up beside him.

"Morning," Troy answered with a smile. He leaned over and kissed her. "I need a coffee. Want me to bring you one too?"

"Coffee, you just opened your eyes," Melissa said, still groggy with sleep.

"Yeah, but once I'm up, I'm up." With that, Troy jumped out of bed and stretched. He bounced on his toes shaking himself loose, before he gathered his clothes.

"Make mine a double then," Melissa said, rolling back over in bed, disappearing beneath the duvet.

"Is there any other way to order coffee?" Troy asked, smiling, he bolted from the room and out of the door downstairs without making a sound.

After dropping Rachel off at the Kids' Klub, after she spent the morning begging her mother to let her go, Melissa and Troy went for a walk. They explored the resort, moving through the entire place, having realized they had yet to take in the full range of resort facilities. They found the tennis courts, and football pitches, each crowded with excited groups. Adults and children alike, running around lost in the holiday fun.

By the time they looped around and back to the beach on the north side of the main resort area, they were both more relaxed and feeling the holiday spirit. They walked hand in hand, their bodies pressing together.

The screams coming from the beach shattered the false imagery that had clouded their minds.

***

With the rest only just waking up, Troy walked back to the chalet with two large coffees in his hand. His mind replaying the events of the night before, when the ground began to shake.

The rumble began deep underground, travelling towards the surface. It cracked open, cutting its path through layer after layer of rock and deposits, built up through the years. The chamber that housed the beast shook, the walls crumbling as the cracks reached it, emptying out into nothing. Chunks of rock the size of car doors fell away and crashed into the reservoir.

The beast stirred, its slumber disturbed. The body woke slowly, a minor movement, a motion barely befitting the word. Slowly, the creature stretched. It could sense the escape, a root to freedom was coming.

Deep down in the earth, a great beast thrashed its tail and crushed the rock around it. It thrashed and the walls broke down. A new tremor began, spreading through the earth at a slow march. Inch by inch, mile by mile, the beast moved towards the surface, and the world it had left behind too long ago.

**

The sea held a deep pink shade long before Troy and Melissa got sight of the source. Around them people screamed. People ran, lost to blind panic, and a great many people bent over double and vomited between their feet.

To find the source of the panic, all they needed to do was follow the trail created by the snake of intestines floating on the tide.

The man was in the surf, sitting propped up on his elbows. People stood around him staring, frozen in place by the shock of the scene. The man was staring down at his feet, which were sitting horizontal to one another. His chest heaved rapidly, causing more blood to surge from the missing midsection. His belly was nothing but a cavernous black maw, spilling his insides into the ocean, torn away as his rescuers pulled his body from the waves. The man looked around, his eyes finding Troy and Melissa. He opened his mouth and a gush of blood spewed over his lips. He fell back into the surf, dead.

"Jesus, look," Melissa cried, pointing out to the water where a body floated face down. It bobbed in the water, while all around it fish took tearing bites of bloody flesh from the body. Everybody stared, nobody moved, nobody expecting the corpse to raise its head and start screaming. The woman thrashed in the water, only stopping when a fish rose and tore her throat out in a spray of blood, spit, and seawater.

"Somebody needs to alert management about this. Call the Coast Guard. There is something in the water. Everybody out." Troy took charge, moving in front of the remaining group.

Most people had fled already. They ran up and down the beach, lost to panic. They stumbled and tripped, falling into each other in their terror fuelled escape.

"I already told them. Someone's coming," an out-of-breath voice spoke.

Troy looked and saw a group of employees running down the beach toward them. The group consisted mainly of young women from the reception. The moment their eyes took in the scene, the blood and organs washing up on the white sandy beach, and they dropped to their knees. Vomit soon followed. A few moments later, the medical staff followed, and while they held a stronger constitution, they were not prepared for the devastation that waited for them. The sick bay was already filling with people who had sustained minor injuries. Troy heard the medical staff mention lost toes and fingers, small scale amputations compared to the carnage of the beach.

"We need to leave," Troy turned and spoke to Melissa.

"I can't believe that asshole isn't here," Melissa replied. She was pale and sweaty. Focusing on the resort manager kept her from collapsing. She heard what Troy said, but could not bring herself to respond.

"Hey, hey, listen, we need to stay focused on this. Let's go collect Rachel. My first concern is getting the two of you away from this resort." Troy took a gentle hold of Melissa's shoulders. "Everything will be alright. I promise."

"Yeah, okay, good idea. Rachel is with the Kids' Klub again. I guess we should go to their clubhouse and collect her from there. The ferry will leave soon … I think … I don't know actually. I just made that up. That bastard isn't even here. Fucker," Melissa spat as her mind spun in a hundred different directions.

"He will get his. We will make sure of it. For now, let's get people out of here." Troy lead Melissa up the beach, breaking into a run the moment they broke through the reassembled mass of onlookers, their morbid curiosity greater than their terror at such a distance.

CHAPTER 11

Rachel followed the group, hanging towards the back. Until now, the Kids' Klub offered her the perfect escape. She loved the arts and crafts activities, especially the tie-dye. That was still something she wanted to do once she got back home. Today was different, however. Today, she was scared. After having seen what happened to her mother and Troy the day before, she no longer held any interest in the water, being near it, on it, or in it. She even put away the copy of *Jaws* into her mother's suitcase, unable to face the words on the page as they described the sea and the beast that lived within it.

When the leader of the Klub, a woman called Rosanna, told them that they were going kayaking on the lake behind the main resort, everybody cheered. Everybody but Rachel.

"If you don't want to go in the water, that is fine. You can stay here with me, but I cannot leave you in the clubhouse, or let you go off on your own. Your mother leaves you in my care, and I just couldn't do it," Rosanna said. She was a young girl, and Rachel thought she was very pretty.

"Please, there are things in the water. They eat people." Rachel didn't know how to find the right words to describe what she had seen.

"I understand your fear. Really I do. We are not going to the sea, we are going to a lake. They built it for the resort. It is nothing more than a big swimming pool. Trust me, you won't find any monsters in the water," Rosanna spoke softly, offering her hand to Rachel, who took it in a vice-like grip.

"I know but … I won't stand by the water," Rachel argued.

"Okay, you don't have to."

Rachel sat by the pier, her knees pulled up to her chest. She hugged herself, watching the others as they paddled and splashed around on the water. She wanted to join them. She wanted to have fun too, but she could not bring herself to out onto the lake. She didn't care what Rosanna said. Monsters were real. The existed, and that meant they could be anywhere.

One of the girls screamed, and Rachel jumped to her feet. The girl's kayak overturned, spilling her into the water. She swam back, laughing, a noise that soon echoed through the entire group.

Rachel could not help feeling stupid. Her heart pounded as she watched, holding her breath as the girl, whose name she could not remember, swam back to her kayak. Kicking her legs, splashing in the water as she tried to pull herself back up on board.

The girl cried out in frustration. She cried out in pain. The water around her began to froth and bubble. White foam turned pink and soon blood fountained into the air as monsters tore the girl apart.

Panic spread among the others, their frantic paddles leaving them off balance. They crashed and collided against one another; several of the weaker kayakers spilled into the water, adding to the general hysteria out on the lake.

From the shore, Rosanna screamed at the group on the water, while the kayak instructor paddled furiously towards the group in a small rowboat. He reached the first of the spilled girls and hauled her into the water. The second, a boy, followed soon thereafter. The severed stump that had once been his leg showered the instructor with blood.

Rachel ran onto the small dock, screaming to the others, telling them to paddle faster. One of the boys broke away from the group, powering his way back toward the dock. He leaped from the boat just as the fish attacked. The fish leaped clear from the water and landed on the seat, its long body filling the craft, while the dangling string of skin hung over the edge. It curled and flapped on its own, like a scorpion's tail. The boat rocked, but did not overturn. The fish thrashed and thrashed, but eventually fell still. The kayak drifted away from the dock and back out into the lake.

A swimmer who had drifted away from the main area of carnage reached the boat and pulled himself out of the water. The cries from those on the shore were lost on his ears, especially when the fish snapped their jaws around the young boy's head, engulfing it, separating it from the rest of the body in a single bite.

Screaming, Rachel paced up and down the dock, watching as the children she considered her friends were slowly ripped apart by the monsters beneath the water.

"Rachel, Rachel, come back here," Rosanna screamed.

Rachel heard her, she turned to move back to the shore, shocked that she had brought herself so close to the edge of the dock.

Something crashed against the dock.

"Help me," a voice cried out.

Rachel recognized Viktor. The only kid younger than her in the Klub; he did not speak much English. Rachel liked him. He was trapped in a kayak. He had been one of a pair in the boat, but all that remained of his older buddy was a puddle of piss on the seat and a bloody handprint on the side of the boat.

Rachel reached out and took his hand. She pulled and helped him out of the boat. The kayak slid away from the dock. Pushed by some force under the water, Viktor was yanked backwards, the boat disappearing from beneath him. He crashed belly first into the water, and dragged the screaming Rachel with him.

They hit the water together and disappeared into the mass of snapping teeth and thrashing bodies.

***

"I don't fucking believe it," Melissa snapped as she read the note on the clubhouse door. "Today of all fucking days, they go into the water."

She paced back and forth, her fists clenching and unclenching as she talked. Her face flashed with anger, but her eyes burned with worry.

"Hey, calm down, we will go and find her. It's on the lake, not the sea. Come on, let's go." Troy put his hands on Melissa's trembling shoulders.

"Where is the lake? I didn't remember seeing it this morning. Where can it be? Oh God, I need to find her." Melissa broke down more and more with each frenzied pace she made.

"Let's go this way. I think I remember seeing something on the map. Besides, the main resort area of this way. They won't make the kids walk for too long to go do something," Troy reasoned.

He tried his best to keep his own raging emotions under control, his fears extending beyond Rachel's safety, and Melissa's wellbeing, to the general problems on the park. His head hurt, his hands throbbed. He balanced on the edge of control, never more than a heartbeat away from breaking down into a frantic wreck. He needed to keep things together.

Melissa walked without too much opposition. She had fallen quiet, her hands clenched within one another. She rubbed at them as if she were auditioning for the role of Lady Macbeth.

They soon found signs directing them to the lake. It was all very well directed, if you actually looked at the boards that were stationed at every junction.

They heard the screams before the lake came into view. Breaking into a run, with Melissa outpacing Troy as the lake came into view, their eyes focused on the massacre at its core.

A group of kids were huddled together on the grass, weeping. They shook from side to side and paid little attention to anything going on around them. Rosanna stood on the bank, pacing up and down frantically, peering into the water every few steps. Further out, three occupied kayaks and a single row boat huddled together as if seeking shelter from a storm. Blood smeared the side of the boat, which bobbed back and forth on the rough surface. Suddenly, something thrust the boat to one side. It jolted violently and pitched over, casting the man into the lake. He was attacked immediately. He screamed and scrambled, trying desperately to pull himself back into the boat, but he failed. Screaming, he thrashed in the water, trying to make it back to his craft. Each time, his attempts became weaker and weaker, until he fell silent and disappeared from view.

"Rachel," Melissa called, striding towards the huddling children. "Rachel, where are you?"

Troy reached Melissa. She turned to him, tears streaming down her face. "She's not here. Where is she? Where's my baby girl?" she questioned, all but sinking to the floor at Troy's feet.

"I'll talk to the others. You sit here," Troy began, but Melissa refused.

"No, I'm going to find her." She moved off towards the lake.

Troy followed close behind.

"Where's my daughter, where's Rachel?" Melissa shot at the young girl, who looked equally frayed and frantic as anybody else by the lake.

"I don't know," the voice replied. "She was here, but then she … she helped pull … and then … oh God, what's happening?" The girl stopped her pacing and fell to the floor. She pulled her knees close to her chest, wrapped her arms around legs and wailed.

Troy moved away, looking into the water.

Something caught his eye, floating just beneath the jetty. He bent down for a closer look. The body floated into view; first a hand, followed by the tanned arm it connected to. Reaching, he grasped it gently within his own, and pulled, using just enough force to bring the body out from under the jetty.

He caught the gasp in this throat, but shot to his feet with enough force that it became a jump. The wooden jetty creaked from the movement.

"What is it, have you found her?" Melissa fired off her questions as she moved.

"No, Melissa, wait. You don't want to —" Troy tried to stop her, but Melissa pushed by him. She moved onto the jetty, peered into the water, and let loose a scream filled with as much pain and sorrow as the human voice can build. It was the cry of a breaking heart, or the walls of existence coming crumbling down.

Rachel's small, lifeless body floated out from under the dock. Melissa fell to her knees, retching and vomiting. The fish had eaten Rachel's face, the flesh all but gone. Only a wet wad of skin and muscle remained over her right cheek, and her lower lip, with the rest was stripped away. Her long hair was flayed out in the water like a saint's corona.

"Melissa, I'm so sorry," Troy said. He reached out a hand and placed it on Melissa's shoulders. He felt her flinch.

She spun around to face him. Her eyes burned with rage, and her face set like thunder. "Get off me," she snarled.

Over Troy's shoulder, her eyes focused on the weeping Rosanna. "You." Melissa advanced.

"Melissa, don't," Troy began, but his words fell on deaf ears. Melissa covered the ground and launched herself at the resort employee.

"You killed her. I left her in your care, and you fucking killed her." Melissa was feral, she scratched and clawed at the defenceless Rosanna. Too weak with shock, she barely registered the onslaught of a devastated mother.

Melissa drew blood as her nails raked down the side of Rosanna's face. Behind them, surviving children began to scream. They stared at Melissa, terrified. It was only when Troy grabbed her and pulled her away from Rosanna, that the young woman began to scream. Melissa struggled and fought against Troy. He moved his arm around her front, bringing it up under her chin. If needed, he would choke her out. He didn't want to, but he was out of options.

It didn't come to it. Melissa's screams and struggles became slaps and sobs. She collapsed to the floor, Troy's arms catching her. He turned her around and pulled her against him. She clung to him as if he were the only thing left in the world.

"I'm sorry, I'm sorry," he whispered over and over, gracing Melissa's forehead with a gentle kiss.

Troy turned around, turning Melissa away from the lake, so she would not have to watch as ravenous fish dragged her daughter's body down into the depths.

The kids stared at them. Rosanna crawled her way over to them and sat in their midst. They clung to her as if she was their mother.

"What on earth? Is everybody alright?" a voice called across to them.

Troy looked and saw a man running towards them. He held a shotgun in his hands. He wore a bright yellow shirt with red palm trees on it, and a pair of equally unsightly shorts. His skin was brown from extensive exposure to the sun and mildly leathered from a lifetime of being near the sea.

"Raul, oh god Raul. Something's happened. There are monsters in the lake, in the sea … everywhere," Melissa managed to spit out. She was the only one who could talk. Even Troy found himself at a loss for words.

"I just left the beach; they are saying it was a shark attack," Raul began.

"It isn't a fucking shark," Troy cut in.

"I know. I found one of those things in the water. It did not make any sense, but it sure as heck ain't no shark," Raul said, moving closer to Troy, his voice lowering.

"The kids need to stay away from the water, we have to bring them back to the resort, to their families. We need to call people down here. Close the whole place down if we must," Troy ordered. He had found his voice and found comfort in taking charge.

"Those things are in the water. We can keep everybody inside, by the hotel. We can figure out what the hell is going on, and try to find a way to resolve it," Raul offered a counter proposal. He was sure of himself, and stood tall. In that moment, the haphazard, easy-going character fell away, and a serious man emerged from beneath it.

"I know where they came from," Troy answered.

"Where?"

"Underground. I was out by the reef, on the ocean side. I found a trench, a deep one too. I got attacked by one of those things. It came from inside the trench," Troy told him. Raul listened and nodded.

"Help me with this lot. Then we need to talk," Raul said, not waiting for an answer before he turned started hustling the survivors away, back towards the hotel.

Troy placed his arms around Melissa, and guided her back the way they came, following the others as best they could.

The hotel area looked like a scene from a newsreel after a bombing or some such incident. Large groups of people huddled together, blood spattered and dirty. The air was pungent with the scent of fear, while the general echo of sobs seemed to whip around them like a winter wind. The resort had come to a halt. Nobody swam, nobody lounged on the sunbeds.

Troy soon learned more people had been attacked, along the beach and all the way down the island to the reef. Six people had died, including three on the reef. The news about the attack on the pool only added to the obvious stresses of the staff. The young, predominantly party-minded group, now found themselves tasked with finding the parents of those that died on the lake, approaching them with the worst piece of news a person could ever receive.

After talking to the medical staff, Raul getting them ahead of the line thanks to a casual friends-with-benefits relationship he had going on with two of the three nurses, they agreed Melissa needed something to calm her down. They gave her a shot and together Raul and Troy took her up to one of the hotel suites. They were unoccupied, and as of yet unavailable to the public.

Placing her in the bed, they sat together and looked out over the resort. The enormous upper floor rooms looked out over both sides of the resort. The two men chose to sit with a sea view before them. Neither spoke. They drank a fancy brand of bottled water and sat staring at the ocean.

Another day in paradise, a rich blue sky leading down to the dazzling cool of the water. To look at it, nobody would know what bloodshed had occurred that day.

"Tell me about that crack," Raul said, starting the conversation just before the silence between them became awkward.

"What? Oh, right, the crack. Well, it is pretty much what it sounds like. A huge crack in the seabed. My best guess would put it at about three meters wide. When I was out there, I got attacked by this, this creature. Nothing but body and teeth. More teeth than anything needs to have in its mouth. It came from inside the trench, I know it did." Troy worked his way through everything that had happened.

"The guy that runs this place is a cocksucker. He should have acted the minute that first guy got attacked. He would rather turn a profit than give two fucks for the safety of those staying here." Raul got up and walked to the window. He pulled out of pack of

Marlboros, pulled one out and lit it. "I guess you don't want one, not with a big championship fight coming your way."

"You recognize me?" Troy stood up and moved to the window.

"I live here alone. Got a lot of free time. The fights give me something enjoyable to watch. For the rest, it is just crazy-assed gameshows and daytime soap operas," Raul laughed.

"You know, I don't think I will ever accept the fact that people recognize my face. I'll pass on the smoke, thanks. You don't seem like the rest of the people on the resort," Troy said.

"I'm not. Technically, I don't work for the resort. I'm a private contractor. They keep me around for the tourists, but have no direct control over me. I got a pretty sweet deal," Raul answered with a smile.

"What do you think is going on out here?" Troy lowered his voice even further. Even though Melissa had been knocked out with enough drugs to keep her asleep until Christmas, it still seemed like the right thing to do.

"Honestly?"

"Of course."

"I think you are correct. They built this island from the seabed up. It makes sense to assume that while they were drilling its foundations, they broke something. Some crack in the earth. Those things out on the water, they do not belong here. I only got a short look at them, but they looked like a sort of viperfish or dragonfish. Only ... the ones I used to study were only a few inches long, six on average." Raul scratched at his face while he spoke. He looked exhausted.

"Study? Is that part of the diving training now?" Troy asked, picking up on the word.

"No, no, God no. I was a marine biologist for the Gulf Bay Maritime Institute. I got sick, cancer, and well, that opened my eyes to the length of life, and I realized I did not want to spend it in a lab. I love the water, it is the one place on Earth that just feels like home, you know? So I quit, packed up my desk, and moved down to Mexico. I fell in love with this stretch of coastline and have worked here ever since."

"These fish, dragonfish, or what you called them. They are native to these waters?" Troy leaned forward against the window.

"No, well, kind of. They are deep water fish. I'm talking deep ocean, around five thousand feet. But those things out in the water, they are not ordinary fish. This one I found came close to three feet in length. The teeth remind me of the dragonfish. Larger, but in keeping with the body size. The only thing I can think of is that these are some older variant of the species. Something almost prehistoric." Raul smiled as he spoke.

"Prehistoric, as in dinosaurs?" Troy couldn't help but scoff.

"I know it sounds crazy, but I do not know of any sort of fish that size and that fucking ugly. Look at the incidents around here. The earthquakes, the tremors, the attacks. It all adds up to something." Raul's face paled as he spoke.

"What can we do?" Troy asked.

"Us, nothing. We need to leave, put as much distance between us and this place as we can before anything else happens. Who knows what else is down in that trench. I mean, if they could exist underground for what, maybe even millions of years, that must mean there is an ocean or something underground. If that is the case, then who knows what else could have survived." Raul returned his gaze to the ocean.

"I don't think anything could survive being trapped together with those things," Troy said, as the image of the destruction caused by the beasts continued to play in his mind.

'That is exactly my point. Imagine if something else did survive, then it is bigger and badder than these things." Raul's stared at Troy, allowing the time for his point to filter through.

"Good God."

"Exactly."

The two men slipped back into silence, contemplating the ramifications of their musings. While they thought, the sun continued its march across the sky. The pandemonium from earlier in the day was now a distant memory. A strange, eerie lull fell over the park, giving everything a slightly haunted feel. The empty pool and abandoned beaches, towels and belongings left behind in the rush for safety.

The haze created by the descending sun hung over the rest like a fog, a physical manifestation of the fear that corralled everybody inside their holiday chalets.

At intervals during the day, both Troy and Raul made trips outside, venturing to their respective lodgings to gather the necessaries to make their escape. The silence of the resort was daunting. The way curtains twitched as they walked by made them feel like the unwanted strangers in town. The silent stares of terrified eyes that followed them from the windows had each man longing for the safety of their confined residence.

"I heard that they arranged for the ferry to make an early morning run. It will load up and take away as many people as possible. They have closed to new arrivals and will have this place empty by the end of the day," Raul said when he returned from his second trip outside.

"That's about bloody time. What are they going to do about the problem itself?" Troy asked, knowing that Raul had connections within the hotel staff.

"They are calling in the government. No idea who, but they are taking it seriously now. The news reached the parent company and suddenly the manager of this place is under pressure to sort things out." Raul sat down and pulled a beer out of his bag. He offered one to Troy, which he took with a smile.

"So I guess this nightmare is over. We just pack up, go home and what, forget it happened? What about Melissa? How can she just wake up and go on tomorrow?" Troy asked, ready to admit that his feelings for Melissa had grown exponentially, and the thought of losing her terrified him.

"I don't know, we just need to focus on getting off this island. The rest, we just have to take one day at a time, I guess."

They sat back on their respective couches, enjoying the silence, giving their minds a chance to settle. Sure enough, both men fell asleep. Overlooking the ocean, neither man was able to resist slumber's relaxing pull. At least, not until the world began to shake.

CHAPTER 12

The creature squeezed its gargantuan frame through the ground. It's multitude of razor sharp teeth cut through the earth and rock as the creature rode the wave of pressure building behind it.

The earth trembled with fear as it rose, and so it should. The beast would rule the seas and terrify the earth.

Once, it had reigned supreme in the ocean. Never more than but a few of its kind came into existence. They left behind no fossils, and an ancestral line so faint, nobody would make the link.

The surface grew closer still. It could taste the apprehension of those that lived in the water, their fear being as cold as their blood. It seeped through the seabed, and the beast ate it up.

It was growing tired, its body weak from being out of the water, but it had more than enough strength to make it. A rest would be required after it broke through, but then, then it would begin its reign as the ultimate predator.

In the past, it had faced larger creatures than itself, but they had fallen, the way everything had fallen to its kind. In a time when the cold northern waters, and its crabs the size of Volvos, had been a plentiful food source, the creature had eaten at will. Now, it would do the same.

The earth split, and water surged around the creature. The cold water from behind was its home for so many millennia. It rushed over its body and into the warmer ocean that stood ready to accept it.

The ground shook and rumbled, radiating out for miles and miles, sending walls of water charging in all directions.

The small school of tuna could sense something. They changed their direction the moment the water around them began to change. It churned and mixed with an icy blast that slowed their bodies down. They drifted.

The creature's mouth burst into the world, open and hungry. The powerful jaws snapped shut, swallowing the entire school whole. The fish struggled and thrashed, as the sharp-pointed secondary teeth within the creature's mouth skewered them. The deep serrated edges cut through the tunas muscular flesh with ease. Their bodies fell apart in a wash of blood and filtered sea water.

Blood seeped through the monster's gills as it swallowed its meal and went off in search of more.

The warm water on the surface made for easy movement and so its strength returned fast. It had already found its next target, and with its children around it, no creature in the sea could stop them.

CHAPTER 13

The rumble that shook the hotel sent the pictures clattering from the walls in the upper-level suite. The table and chairs rattled on the floor like loose change atop the washing machine during a spin cycle.

Troy fell from the sofa as he rolled over in surprise at the commotion. Wrenched from sleep, he was momentarily lost; dazed and confused.

Things became clearer when Raul went running to the window. Troy moved to his side as the jet of water shot into the air. He could not be certain, but he was sure he also caught sight of something monstrous as it rose up and then came crashing back down into the ocean.

"What the hell was that?" Troy asked.

"I have no idea, but it is a little bigger than the creatures we spoke about last night." Raul looked at him. His face had paled, and his eyes bulged in their sockets. "Hold on."

The wall of water rushed towards the resort, sweeping over the beach and up onto the boardwalk. The torrent continued to move, washing everything away. It hit the buildings and the hotel with enough force to shake the structure to its foundations. When the building did not fall, the tide simply pushed the water around it, surging even harder through the paths.

When it was over, and the surge calmed down, the resort was underwater. It was hard to tell how deep from so high up, but judging from the surroundings, it looked to be submerged close to knee deep.

"What do we do now?" Troy asked, staring at Raul in disbelief.

"We have to get away. Get to the ferry, let the authorities handle this," Raul answered.

"I'll go wake Melissa; you gather as much as possible. We are going to grab anything and everything we can find." Troy took charge.

Melissa was already awake when he walked into the room. Standing by the window, she scratched at her neck, the skin already turning angry and red. She tried to hide her sobs, but her whole body seemed to vibrate, as Troy placed a hand on her shoulder.

"We need to leave," he whispered.

"No, I can't leave her," Melissa cried, her voice tiny. It sounded flat and defeated.

"Melissa, you need to leave. This place is not safe. Rachel would not —" Troy began, but Melissa spun around on him.

"Don't you dare say that. Don't you dare." She collapsed into his arms, weeping and wailing. She clenched her fists over his shirt, tearing at the skin of his shoulders.

Her body turned rigid, her grip powerful. Troy said nothing. He waited, and without warning, the fight drained from her. Melissa fell into him, defeated. Breathing heavily, and sobbing gently, she allowed Troy to lead her from the bedroom and into the main area of the suite. Raul stood waiting for them, a few meagre supplies in his hands.

"They don't really stock much in the way of survival," he said, holding up the flashlight and water bottles. "I had more at my place, but no chance it survived that tsunami."

"It will have to do. Let's get to the blasted ferry and leave this godforsaken island." Troy took charge, and with Melissa leaning against him, they left the room and headed down to the ground floor.

The lift shut down the moment the building began to shake. It was a built-in safety feature. The fact that there seemed to be people in it made no difference. As Troy, Raul, and Melissa made their way down the stairs, all twenty-six flights in the thirteen-story building, they could hear the terrified cries of the people trapped in the lift come echoing through the walls.

The large lobby was underwater, only ankle deep, but enough to topple the plants and more lightweight decorations. Papers and other small debris floated on the water, which seemed to swirl through the building, searching for a way back out to the where the real party could be found.

The glass entry doors were closed. The flood would not be stopped, however, as water leaked through the seal of the left- and right-hand glass panels. The rotating door was also flooded, moving like a waterwheel, turning more and more as each opened segment drained into the lobby.

They could see no sign of any members of staff, or other guests.

"Where is everybody?" he asked.

"Either hiding, or already on their way to the ferry dock," Raul answered.

They moved slowly, reacting to every sound. Something crashed against the door. Troy spun around as a sun lounger from the pool area floated out of view.

"I guess we just have to walk?" Troy said, as they stood by the glass doors.

"We need to find a way to the ferry. Higher ground is what we need. If we could make it across to the beach area, we could even grab the jet skis," Raul suggested, speaking in quiet, thought-heavy tones.

"Jet skis?" Troy coughed.

"Yeah, they arrived earlier in the week. People can hire them and go out for an hour or so. They haven't been used yet, but I helped unload them a few days ago."

"But that would mean we have to go back to the beach. Where those things are," Melissa spoke up. Her voice distant but defiant. She did not look at the men, but kept her gaze focused on the world beyond the hotel.

"True, but this water could have swept them everywhere. We can always try it on foot, maybe try to take a car. A few of the guys who work on the beach drive four-by-fours. They are parked across the way." Raul pointed to the right.

"Or we sit here and wait for the authorities. They have to send the Coast Guard or something, right?" Melissa spoke again, her words beginning to take on more substance.

"It is possible, but well, whatever caused this flood must have been big. If it came from underground, like the others, then we are talking big, big. A scale unlike anything we can comprehend. I wouldn't want to be sitting here if that thing decides to come for a closer look," Raul said.

"Okay, I say we make a break for the cars. The water cannot be this deep all over the island. We make it to the cars, drive a way, and if that doesn't work, we turn around and come back and try the jet ski option," Troy decided, once again stepping into the role of leader.

"We do this on three. One, two, three." Raul and Troy pulled and the glass doors parted.

The force of the rushing water aided them in opening the doors. The flood surged towards them, almost knocking Melissa off her feet. Troy reached out and held her stable. Fighting against the current, they stepped outside and were welcomed into Hell.

The sound of people's shrieks and cries of help echoed around the resort. To their left, a group of people waded through the water, holding their belongings above their heads. Suitcases loaded with clothes and holiday paraphernalia that just could not be left behind. The four adults, two men and two women, each pale from exertion, refused to drop their belongings. Even when the first woman was tugged beneath the water, and the surface stained red with her blood, they continued to clutch their belongings.

The second man fell next. He fell to his knees and spat blood as the creatures ravaged his lower body. He fell forward, landing face first in the water and was instantly set upon by four different creatures. They attacked with a stomach-churning ferocity that forced Troy's group to turn their heads.

"Run," Raul called to the others, and instructed his own group.

Troy and Melissa, whose strength seemed to have returned at the sight of the challenge that lay ahead of them, broke into a run.

Raul was close behind. None needed to turn around as the remaining two holidaymakers fell beneath the water's surface.

"Round the building. To the right," Raul ordered.

They rounded the hotel and crossed the car park. It was mostly staff parking, although a few special guests had brought their own vehicles, an escort bringing them from the ferry to their lodgings. Of course, these people had paid a lot of money for the privilege.

"Quick, onto the roof." Troy pointed up, as something broke the surface to their right.

He helped Melissa up first, and waited for Raul before leaving the water himself. They scrambled onto the bonnet of the large four-by-four, and then up onto the roof. A few moments later, something crashed into the side of the car causing it to rock, and Melissa to scream.

"We will never make it. There's too many of them," Melissa cried.

"Help me," a voice called out.

Troy turned, eventually spotting a young woman in a resort uniform stuck in the car a few spaces away. She wound down the window to call for their attention.

"Wait right there," Troy called, and without warning, jumped down into the water.

He reached the car in a flash, and quickly scrambled up onto the roof, helping the girl through the window and along the way.

"Thank you, thank you, thank you," she said over and over.

"Don't mention it," Troy answered, trying not to grimace as his injured hands burned beneath the bandages.

"Troy, what do we do?" Melissa called to him, her voice filling with panic.

"Just hang in there. We need to make it across the carpark. The jeeps are not far. The water looks shallower, too. It barely reaches the tops of their wheels," Troy replied, squinting at the row of cars parked beneath a row of palm trees.

"Looks like they are blocked in," Raul said, his keen eyes also catching the felled palms.

"Yeah, well, we cross that bridge when we come to it," Troy said. "Let's worry about that after we actually reach them. We should be able to move over the cars."

"What?" the young woman shrieked.

"Yeah, it's easy. We can at least make it half way, you guys, too," Troy spoke up, pointing to the two rows of cars, parked neatly beside one another. Troy's route only contained five cars, while Melissa and Raul's path offered seven, bringing them that much closer to the cars. "We shuffle along, one at a time. You guys get in the car and start it up, and I'll move the trees, and clear us a path."

Before anybody could question the plan again, a large shadow flashed in the water, crashing against Troy's car. The young woman screamed and threw herself at Troy, wrapped arms around him.

"Hey, hey, it's okay. What's your name?" Troy asked.

"Maria," the young girl cried. She could not have been long out of her teens.

"Listen to me, Maria, you can do this. It's just like using stepping stones to cross a river. You must have done that before right?" Troy tried hard to hide the urgency in his voice. Ahead of them, Melissa had made the jump to the first car, and Raul followed close behind.

Maria nodded her head, but did not speak.

"Okay, then this will be a piece of cake. Come on, let's go together." Troy took her hand and helped her jump.

Together, the four of them made to the end of the rows of parked cars. Raul had almost slipped on their fifth jump, but had managed to catch his balance at the last minute.

"Okay, you guys get to the cars, and start them up. Maria, I want you to join them. I'll clear those trees and be right behind you," Troy instructed, giving orders without faltering.

Melissa looked at him to offer an argument, but she said nothing. They had no other options. Raul jumped from the car, landing in the water with a loud splash. It was shallower than at the start, but still deep enough for the fish to swim.

Melissa followed him, and they ran, splashing to the car. The doors were unlocked and they jumped inside, closing them behind them.

"Do we go?" Maria asked.

"Not yet, give it a second. Let the water settle," Troy instructed.

"No, no, we can make it now," the girl said, jumping from the top of the red sedan they stood perched upon.

"Maria," Troy called, trying to stop her.

Maria landed running, her feet twisting as she hit the water. Her legs went out from under her and she crashed face first into the water. Troy looked around and caught sight of three shadows darting through the water. They sped towards Maria, hunting her down.

Maria broke the surface, and pushed herself to her feet. She slipped and fell back to her knees. Moving to stand once more, she froze, and screamed, blood spreading in the water. Turning, she stared at Troy, fumbling at the fish that was half-buried in her gut. She spun around and around, as if trying to shake it loose, but all she succeeded in doing was casting droplets of blood and small pieces of meat in the water like chum.

Without thinking, Troy jumped down from the car and ran towards the woman. Troy grabbed the fish and pulled it free, tearing an even larger hole in her stomach. The fish thrashed around in his hands, long strips of flesh dangling from its clenched jaws.

Maria continued to scream, while her gut leaked blood and bile from her ruptured liver. Troy swung the struggling fish, knocking it against the side of a car. The metal door caved inwards, but the fish continued to fight. He swung again, and again. His hands burned, but his rage burned brighter. Maria collapsed to her knees, pitching forward into the water, and still Troy swung the now-dead fish. Its head cracked open after the sixth swing. Loose teeth went flying along with gills, blood, and cold globs of mashed tissue.

"Troy!" Melissa screamed his name, her voice shattering the red mist cocoon that had settled around him.

Troy looked up and dropped the fish. His arms fell to his sides, tired from the exertion. Blood soaked his bandaged hands, both his own and Maria's. Her body floated by, face down, drifting away from them all. Troy became aware of something in the water. It shot past him, narrowly missing his left leg. The fish attacked Maria, wrenching at her body.

Troy moved. He ran.

Sprinting to the car, he pushed at the trees blocking their path, clearing a space large enough for the vehicle to fit through. The engine revved before Troy moved the last tree. Raul stopped, or rather, slowed down just enough to let Troy jump inside.

The car sped along through the water, which dropped to little more than ankle deep as they sped away from the hotel.

"Fuck that was close," Raul said, panting.

"You are telling me," Troy answered. "So tell me, Mr. Hooper. What did you make of those things?"

Raul looked back at Troy and smiled. "Very cute," he answered. "I think they are definitely a species of dragonfish. The lure hanging from their jaw, and the phosphoric effect on their flank, the resemblance is strong. Especially when they sped through the water."

"So you know what these things are?" Melissa asked. Having missed their earlier conversation, her voice held an accusing tone.

"Not exactly. It's a long story, but we think those things are an ancient species, let loose as a result of the earthquakes." Raul stopped talking as he jerked violently on the wheel, avoiding a small school of fish feasting on the remains of a holidaying family.

"I see the ferry," Melissa spoke up from the passenger seat. "I see people, too," she added.

Raul pushed the accelerator to the floor, coming close to flying over the standing water as they bounced and jumped over the debris-strewn road. "Hold on," he said.

The crowded ferry sat low in the water. It was clear that not everybody would not all make it onto the first trip, although nobody seemed willing to accept this. Bodies piled onto the boat, families got torn apart, literally and figuratively, as the more selfish holidaymakers jumped onto the already overcrowded vessel.

The dock was underwater, but nobody paid it any mind, not until the ferry finally closed its doors and pulled away. One unlucky man decided to make a last minute jump for the boat, just as the cargo doors finished their ascent.

His body burst like a stepped on grape as the heavy metal door shut on him. His legs dangled against the side of the craft for a while, before falling away into the ocean.

The ferry left the dock much to the urgent appeal of those left behind. Raul tried hard to calm them, looking around for more members of staff, or even the resort manager, who should have been the one direction things in the event of a tragedy.

"I don't believe him. That cowardly motherfucker," Raul snarled as he re-joined Troy and Melissa.

"What?" she asked.

"That son of a bitch manager, I bet he made sure that he was one of the first people on the boat. He just cut his losses and ran."

"Well, I guess all we can do now is wait. Let's move to higher ground, as long as we stay out of the water, then we can wait it out." Troy pointed to a spot of higher ground that would keep them dry until the ferry returned.

Screams began to sound as they made their way up and out of the water. They tried to take the remaining survivors with them, but more refused. They were all too focused on the ferry. They watched as their salvation sailed away, collectively hoping for it to return as quickly as possible.

The fish moved in, snatching people where they stood. Bones snapped and limbs were severed in a bubbling fountain of blood and gore. The younger people in the pack fell first, their meat the sweetest and the softest.

People ran, they screamed, and they fell, knocked to the floor by their panicking neighbours only to be trampled by those that came behind.

"What happened?" Melissa asked.

"People are panicking," Raul answered. He and Troy watched the remaining throng of holidaymakers as they ran around in the middle of the massacre, all idea of order lost to them.

"No, I mean to the boat." She pointed out to the sea, where the ferry appeared to be listing heavily to one side.

"No, no, it can't," Raul spat as his eyes fell upon the stricken vessel.

CHAPTER 14

The beast was hungry. It had travelled far enough without feeding. It propelled its enormous body through the water, staying low to the bed, its belly scraping over the stones and reefs. After spending so long in captivity, stuck in a pool it soon outgrew, the feel of the open ocean was foreign to it. It needed the closeness of the seabed.

The creature sensed its prey. He could feel the impulses moving through the water, and it could sense the disturbance that his passage caused.

Rising from the depths, it charged at its larger prey. The beast knew it would put up a good fight, and the reward would be great. Even in its simple mind, the creature understood the relationship between a big fight and a large meal.

With its jaws closed, the beast rammed its prey, hitting it low on the left and side.

The ferry lurched heavily to one side, and fell still in the water. Something cut at the beast's flesh, the swirling tail of the beast, but a swift thrash from its mighty tail rendered the propellers unless, and turned the battle in favour of the beast.

Food dropped into the water like raindrops, as they leaped from the sinking ship, favouring their chances in the ocean. They were picked apart by the beast's children. They swam by its side, straying only far enough to feed before returning to its flank.

They struck fast, their lures twitched and struck out, skewering their prey, bringing it to their mouths. The passengers from the ferry never stood a chance. Most never saw their attackers, and those that did, did not live long enough to process the images.

The beast circled down to the seabed and charged again. Powerful contractions pushed its body through the water. It rose like a missile, leaving the water to arch its body around and crash down onto its foe. To the beast, it made no difference if its prey was made of flesh and blood, or iron and steel. It had fought and defeated tougher beasts in its time.

The ferry's iron shell bent and buckled. The people packed onto its already-listing deck were crushed by the massive body that collapsed onto them. A least a hundred feet long, the body crushed the boat, snapping it through the middle.

The two halves began to sink and the ocean came alive as the smaller creatures took flight. They leaped from the water, landing on the sinking deck. Their bodies thrashed and pushed them along, while their lures struck out at anything within range. Everybody that fell into the water met their end in a flash of teeth and the echoing screams of death.

*****

Troy put his arm around Melissa and she pulled herself close to him. She wept as the boat sank. They stood in silence. All around them, bodies fell and people ran amok, screaming, shouting, and shoving each other out of the way, sacrificing their neighbour in order to guarantee their own survival.

"That thing … it looked like a whale, or something," Troy said, unable to conjure up an image of any sea creature large enough to fit what he had seen.

"It was a monster, a beast from the oceans of Hell. We can't trust the sea, it is no longer safe," Raul said, his eyes watching the sea. "Such creatures should not exist. It is not possible for them to exist."

"What do you mean?" Melissa asked.

"I mean, I believe those creatures have been trapped underground for millions of years. They should not be able to survive in the conditions our oceans present," Raul said, clarifying his statement.

"I understand, but is no way they can actually be millions of years old," Melissa pointed out.

"The world is a mysterious place," Raul answered. "There are many events throughout history that cannot be rationally explained."

"So we head back to the hotel, and call the Coast Guard? There has to be a way for us to leave this fucking place," Troy said, looking at the group.

"That sounds like the best option, but I have no idea how far we would get," Raul answered.

At that moment, the vehicle's engine roared to life. Troy and Raul spun around to watch as a group of survivors piled into the waiting car. The car sped off with at least nine people shoved into the car, and a further three holding onto the roof. Two of them fell off the moment the car made a sharp left turn to try and avoid a half-eaten corpse that blocked the road. They landed with a splash, and never resurfaced. The car showed no sign of stopping for their lost companions, speeding off into the jungle, heading along the wrong road, as if returning to the hotel.

"Great, what do we do now? We won't make it walking, and I doubt we would have much luck roping and riding a couple of sea turtles." Troy looked around, his arms out in gesticulation.

"I have no idea," Raul said, defeated.

"Hey, it's me," Melissa's spoke up, suddenly.

Troy spun around, expecting to find a newcomer approaching their group. It shocked him to see Melissa talking into a cell phone.

"Yes, I know, I'm sorry I called, but I just really need your help, and I don't know who else I can turn to." Melissa wept openly, giving in to the grief.

She said nothing else, but hung up the phone. Turning, she looked at Troy, and he too wanted to weep. Her sadness, too great to be contained, swept over him like a cloud.

"Who was that?" Raul asked.

Melissa looked at them both for a moment before eventually answering, "My ex-husband."

CHAPTER 15

Captain James Andrews was asleep in his cabin when the phone began to ring. He woke with a jolt, but the second his feet hit the floor, his mind cleared, leaving him ready for action. A lifetime of service in the military had made the journey from sleep to wakefulness a swift one.

"Captain Andrews," he barked into the phone.

"Sir, it's Aiden, we just got a message from Norfolk, I think you need to come to the bridge," Aiden Quinn, his XO's, voice spoke. It sounded tinny over the internal phone system, which could not have been further from the truth when heard in person.

"I'll be right there," Andrews said, half-dressed before his XO replaced the receiver.

At five in the morning, the skyline above the Atlantic held the energizing glow of early morning promises. It gave some much-needed separation to the darkness of both the night sea and sky.

Peace and tranquillity ruled the bridge, as DESRON seventeen returned home after running shakedown manoeuvers out in the mid-Atlantic. As per the captain's orders, they operated on a skeleton watch. They were home, and in friendly waters. Everybody had deserved the chance to grab a few extra hours off-duty. Andrews ran a tight ship, but he was a fair captain.

"Sir," Aiden spoke, approaching his captain.

"What's the news, Mr. Quinn?" Andrews asked, looking around for the sign of a cup of coffee.

"I just got a call from Norfolk. Something strange is happening down on the Mexican coast. Reports of a lot of casualties on a resort down that way. They said somebody attacked them, and sunk a ferry boat."

"Jesus, are they thinking terrorists?" Andrews asked.

As Quinn answered, a young seaman arrived holding two cups of steaming hot coffee. He gave one each to the senior officers and disappeared back into the peripheral.

"They don't know yet. Everything is unconfirmed. We are about three hours out and they want us to be on the lookout. Apparently, they are in talks with the Mexican authorities, offering help. The resort is an island. Manmade kind of deal. Built and operated by a US company." Quinn relayed the few snippets of information he had received.

"Thank you, Mr. Quinn; open up a line to Norfolk, I want to talk to the commandant," Andrews ordered their radio technician. With coffee in hand, he could handle anything life threw at him.

Aiden had served with Andrews his entire career, starting out in the Navy when he first left college, slowly working his way up to the position he had now. It made him proud to have been able to follow his captain for so many years, but he also appreciated that the captain's days were running down, and a successor would need to be promoted, somewhere.

Aiden moved to follow when suddenly his phone began to ring. The satellite phone connected to the mainland, but was not supposed to be used, except in times of emergency. He looked at the screen, and his hands began to shake. Only one other person had his number.

"Melissa, what's wrong? Is it Rachel?" Aiden asked, as several crew members turned in his direction at the sound of his worried voice.

"Aiden, I don't know where you are, but I have nobody else to call. We are trapped, on a resort, Tropicana Island," Melissa spat the words, speaking fast, wanting to deliver as much information as she could before they lost reception. It was something Aiden taught her the day she announced her pregnancy.

"What, where?" he interrupted.

"Down in Mexico, oh God Aiden, I don't know what to do. We are trapped. There are too many of them. The water is infested. They are killing everybody." The signal crackled, and the rebounded cell call growled and feedback static every minute or so.

"Okay, stay calm. Just stay calm. Who is attacking you? Can you describe them?" Aiden probed, asking the questions his endless hours of training drills required of him.

"Yes, yes, but it's not like you are thinking," Melissa said.

"Then what is it? Come on, Mel, tell me everything," he asked.

***

"Giant what?" Captain Andrew's exclaimed.

The two men had retreated to the captain's ready room where they indulged in a second cup of surprisingly good coffee. Melissa explained everything that had happened to Aiden. It sounded crazy as she explained it to him, and now, as he relayed the messaged to his CO, it sounded downright ludicrous.

"Giant fish. Prehistoric fish. I know it sounds insane, but Melissa, she ... she is a serious woman, but whatever happened out there really riled her. She sounded terrified on the phone. I've never heard her like that."

Aiden tried to justify his request, but understood he could not request a DESRON unit would be rerouted to the coast of Mexico on the basis of a phone call from his ex-wife, claiming dinosaur fish had hatched and were terrorizing the ocean.

"Aiden," the captain spoke, placing his coffee on the table. "I trust you, implicitly. This ... this is madness."

"I know it is, but what about the call we got from Norfolk? That all ties together, right?" Aiden pushed, aware of the fine line he was walking, but he had to try.

James Andrews took a deep breath and let out a slow, heavy sigh. "The Mexican Coast Guard is sending a couple of boats out to the source of the attacks," he spoke, the hesitancy clear in his words.

"Where did the reports come from?" Aiden jumped on his CO's words.

"Aiden —" he began.

"They came from the resort, didn't they? Come on, James, don't lie to me. My ex-wife and daughter are on that island. If something is in the water, then sending boats will be like using oil to put out a fire." Aiden studied his CO's face intently.

Captain Andrews said nothing. His eyes seemed fixed on the table.

"Please, sir."

"Alright, you can take a chopper and two men. Head straight to the island, collect your wife and daughter, and hightail is back here. I can keep us still in the water long enough for you to do that." James raised his eyes and stared at his XO. "But Aiden, whatever you find, do not engage. The Mexicans sure don't want any military involvement in their waters, not with everything going on at the moment."

"I understand, thank you, sir." Aiden finished his coffee and left the room, leaving Captain Andrews with the quietly nagging voice of his conscience.

CHAPTER 16

Lieutenant Luiz Abrego had served his country as a member of the Mexican Coast Guard for almost twenty-five years. When his superiors called him and told him to take a boat out and investigate an incident at the Tropicana Resort, he jumped to it. He led two boats into the water with a total of twelve men, himself included.

They were armed with automatic rifles, and a mounted gun on the bow of each boat offered additional firepower. The news of the ferry accident began filtering through just before they left the port. It had them all on high alert. Two-man teams sat behind the mounted guns, while the remaining officers stood along the sides of the boats, their weapons ready to engage whatever threat they came up against.

The island came into the view. The water between them was dotted with debris. As the boats slowed their approach, the first few bodies floated into view.

Beside Luiz, his XO Juan Delgardo made the sign of the cross and bowed his head. "What on earth did that?" he asked as a hollowed-out corpse passed by their boat.

"I don't know, but I want everybody ready to take these things down," Luiz ordered.

The first fish leaped from the water in front of a jumpy young recruit by the name of Pedro Morales, who, starting his second week on the job, still felt out of his depths in the new role. The creature sprang from the water, its teeth snapping at air. At least two feet long, its body was a slimy brown colour. Without thinking, Pedro fired a burst from his M4. The fish's body exploded, as the well-placed rounds tore its body to shreds.

The cries rang out and a domino effect of automatic rifle fire rang out from both boats. The water splashed as if caught in a heavy rain.

"Hold your fire. Hold your fire," Luiz called out, trying to settle his agitated crew. The gunshots fell away and silence reigned. "What the heck?" The same questions murmured from the lips of every crew member.

The fish jumped from the water towards the boats. They buffeted them, causing both crafts to rock and sway. Several larger ones leaped higher, almost jumping onto the deck of the ship.

"Get us out of here," Luiz ordered, giving Juan the controls while he turned to survey the damage.

The giant fish clamped its jaws shut around the hand of one of his men, severing the limb in an instant. The man fell to the floor, the fish with him. The body convulsed and thrashed, somehow pushing itself along the deck.

Two other men turned and opened fire on the creature. The body burst open in a shower of blood, but not before the lure had struck out and skewered the felled man through the heart.

With the attention of a quarter of his crew taken by the events on the boat, they left themselves open to further attacks. More fish jumped, three more landing on the deck.

The impact of their breach made the boat rock. Luis fell forward, crashing against the side of the crude wheelhouse. A warm line of blood trickled down his forehead. Luis wiped it away with the back of his hand. He did not have the time to waste getting treatment for the wound. Their boat turned, swinging around in a tight arc, trying to come around into safer water. Beside them, the second boat struggled to withstand the onslaught. The damaged boat started taking on water in the stern. They were sinking. Fish breached onto the deck, their long dangling lures struck out.

Luiz ran out to the deck, and raising his M4, he opened fire. At the front of the boat, the guns roared into life, spewing hot lead into the water. The froth turned pink, but still the fish came.

The rising swell of larger creatures dented and twisted the metal hulls of both boats, overturning them in quick succession.

The mesh of teeth that protruded from their faces formed a protective sheath over their heads as they crushed the metal.

The boats lifted and turned, pitching everybody on board into the water. The men hit the water screaming as the frenzied attack began, the fish tearing them limb from limb.

Swimming hard, Luiz managed to pull himself onto the overturned hull of his boat. He spun around, looking for any other survivors, but all around him, bodies floated on the water. All were gone in a matter of seconds. Fish had taken his boats, and his crew.

With the sun disappearing beneath the waves, reality set in. Luis shook as shock ravaged his system. He had seen a lot of shit in his years. His time in the Navy had shown him the best and the worst sides of Mexican life. Yet nothing had prepared him for the close proximity of such carnage.

The water calmed, and the loneliness of his situation began to hit home. Luiz moved to adjust his position, and the boat creaked, bobbing in the water. His heart skipped a beat. Beneath him, under the surface, he could feel them moving, circling the boat, waiting for their chance.

A flash of blue light appeared. It was gone in an instant. Then came another, and another, following one another, until it formed a full circle. It was a pulsing blue light, like a neon sign outside a liquor store. Luiz stared at it, peering close at the strangely hypnotic pulse. One of the fish broke from their high-speed patrol, leaping from the water. Its mouth snapped as it rose, teeth slicing at the air with a shrill whoosh.

Luiz jumped back, avoiding the majority of the teeth. A few sliced through the skin of his cheek, but their purchase did not stick, and the creature fell back into the water.

Luiz screamed, his hands reaching for his face. Blood flowed from the three torn puncture wounds. It oozed through his fingers and ran down the hull into the water. His face burned as if on fire. He stood up. The water splashed behind him. Luiz wanted to turn, but his legs gave out. He fell onto the hull, his head cracking against a jagged section of raised metal. He saw stars and tasted blood. He couldn't move. His head was embedded in the torn metal, pinning him in place.

The water around the boat got rougher, only getting worse as the blood flowing from his head wound reached the water.

The boat rocked, and Luiz's body slid this way and that on the blood-slicked deck, pivoting from the point where his skull stuck to the hull. Growing woozy, he thought of his wife. She would be busy making the kids their dinner. He cried out as the first fish tore into the flesh of his thigh. He opened his eyes and saw his home, saw his children playing; his son with a football, his daughter with her dolls. The second bite came and washed the image away. His mind brought him back to the boat, back to the cold reality of his expiration. The large fish jumped clear of the water, its lure shooting out to slice through Luiz's neck. A shower of blood fountained into the air. Luiz closed his eyes and tried to call back the image, but there was nothing but black.

CHAPTER 17

Aiden sat in the co-pilot seat of the SeaHawk helicopter. In the back were two men he had chosen based on their proximity to him when he made his hasty journey towards the helipad.

Corporals Henning and Wyndham sat together listening to the debriefing they received as they took off. Neither man wanted to question their senior officer, even as the story continued to grow more and more bizarre.

"We need to stay sharp. The sun is falling and we are losing visibility by the minute. I reckon we are still an hour out," the pilot spoke to Aiden once the eventual string of questions dried out from the back.

"That's fine. The island is small, manmade in fact. This is just an extraction. We touchdown, grab out targets, and head on back to the ships. Keep your eyes peeled for any signs of trouble. We report everything back to the ship. They will relay it to the folks back home," Aiden said, repeating himself for the umpteenth time, but with the political situation between the US and Mexico even more precariously balanced than usual, he could ill-afford to make a mistake.

"Do you mean something like that?" the pilot asked, pointing out of the window on Aiden's side.

In the distance, flashes of gunfire made the horizon twinkle.

"Exactly like that. Swing us around, I want to come in from the flank," Aiden gave the order, but the pilot was already adjusting their course.

They circled around the island, the devastation readily apparent. The water levels had dropped, revealing the full extent of the damage done by the tsunami. The drone of the rotors cancelled out of the echoing rattle of the gunfight below, but that did not stop Aiden from realizing the fight had suddenly stopped. For a moment, everything fell still beneath them, and then one of the boats disappeared.

"Did you see that?" the pilot asked.

"I did, but are you seeing this?" Aiden asked.

"What the hell is that?" the pilot asked.

Below them, the remaining overturned boat was surrounded by a flickering blue ring, like an electrical current pulsing through the water.

"What kind of weapon does that?" the pilot asked.

"I don't know, but it is too late for them now. Radio it back to the ship, and take us to the island." Aiden fidgeted in his seat. He had a bad feeling about what lay in wait for them.

The helo made a sharp turn and headed back towards the island. They found a place to land close to the main building on the small patch of hand-sculpted. Water pooled around the bird's grounded wheels, but the worst of the flood had subsided. The three men jumped out while the pilot powered the bird down.

"I'll keep her ready for a quick take off. Just give me a sign when you head this way and I will have her purring like a contented kitten for you," he said to Aiden.

"Roger that. Everybody set your times. I want us back here in sixty minutes. Henning, I want you to take the south, Wyndham, start north around behind the hotel and then head south to meet Henning. I'll go inland. You run into any trouble, you holler on the radio. Got it?" Aiden ordered.

"Yes, sir," both men answered in unison.

"Perfect. Remember, we are looking for my ex-wife and my daughter. Melissa and Rachel. Other survivors, we need to make comfortable, bring back to the hotel if necessary. Help is on the way." It hurt Aiden to talk about making people comfortable and then leaving them behind, but the mission was the mission and he could not allow them to stray from it. The consequences were too severe.

The Mexican authorities were on the way, and while he hoped to God they had more planned than the two boats they saw defeated as they flew over, he did not plan on stepping on their toes any more than he had already.

The debris lay strewn everywhere. Deck chairs, towels, plates and cups torn from the now-shattered cafes and poolside bars littered the path. However, it did little to hamper their general movement. Several bodies lay motionless on the ground, and a quick inspection led Aiden to believe they had drowned. The cuts and abrasions to their bodies could be explained by a raging torrent of water. Confirmation of the tsunami had come moments before they left the ship. It had hit the mainland, but the waves had caused little more than an early high tide.

Moving away from the landing zone, the devastation became less; the water pools became larger, but the debris from the resort grew less.

Something splashed in a large puddle to Aiden's left. He looked as the surface rippled. It splashed again, and he caught sight of something. Moving over, he peered into the water and saw the strangest fish he had ever seen before. It was thick and brown with heavy-looking scales. They had been removed in large patches along the things twelve-inch body. It thrashed in the shallow water, the jaws snapping open and shut. One of the eyes had burst, the empty socket staring through the mesh of teeth.

"What the heck?" Aiden spoke aloud, crouching down for a closer look.

The fish responded to his voice, the head raising long enough for a long stand of skin to roll out from under it. A strange barbed end whipped in the air.

Aiden jumped backwards, falling on his ass as he did. The barbed end missed his face by a few inches, but in his mind, it came much closer.

"You're a mean fucker," he said, staring as the fish lashed out once more, the dangling barb curling and stabbing at the air. Its attacks grew weaker, and soon, the fish lay still again.

Pushing on, Aiden began to wonder about what was going on around the island. He came across more bodies and more fish, their carcasses already starting to bloat in the warm evening air. He bent down and picked up one particularly nasty character. It was at least two feet long, and he guessed well over the five kilos. Aiden hoisted it into the air by the tail. Looking at it, the face reminded him of the alien from the film of the same name. Or rather, the smaller creature that emerged from the queen. Its teeth looked razor sharp, and Aiden refused to allow curiosity to get the better of him and touch them.

He had seen images of fish that looked similar to this, but they belonged to the deep, dark part of the ocean, not shallower coastal waters. Aiden let the fish fall to the floor. It landed with a splat. The long barb hung down almost the same length as the body. It looked to be a flap of skin that emerged from under the creature's jaw.

"Help," a weak voice called.

Aiden spun around, his M16 raised and nestled into his shoulder.

At first, he thought he imagined it. Only when the voice called out again did he get a bearing on their position. He moved forward, subconsciously stepping around the large puddles of water. He found the man trapped under a pile of leaves and branches.

"What happened?" Aiden asked, as he began to clear away the debris.

"The water, it just came out of nowhere. I was sitting by the pool, and we just got swept away. Then … then those things came. They ate everybody, just attacked them like wild beasts." The man's body shook with such force it bordered on being a convulsion.

The man had been skewered by a large slice of wood. It entered somewhere in the man's back, and exited just below his belly. The bloodied stump of wood was already tacky. Aiden knew he couldn't remove it. He also knew the man would not survive his injuries. So Aiden cleared a patch of ground, sat down, and took the man's hand in his own.

"It's all going to be alright," he lied.

The man didn't respond, he was already slipping away. Even the rattle of gunfire coming across the island could rouse him.

Aiden jumped to his feet. His orders had been clear. If his team opened fire, then it meant the island was not secure. He tightened his grip on the M16.

The man slipped away without so much as a final sigh. He simply stopped breathing. Aiden said a prayer and walked away.

***

James Wyndham circled around the back of the hotel. He jumped over the larger patches of debris, and forced his way through the water pools. Midway through his third year of service, his career looked bright. He had risen fast, his name spoken in all the right places and for all the right reasons. He moved behind the hotel, sweeping around the building, his rifle raised to his shoulders. There was something about the island. He could not put his finger on it, the only way he could describe it would be a feeling in his gut. He felt as if he were being watched.

He found the first body behind the hotel. Her neck had been snapped, presumably when the water threw her against the hotel wall. Just beyond where she lay, more bodies lay waiting.

James stood over them and looked around. The devastation came into view, as if a mist had lifted from him, his perception of everything changed. The dead came into view. Their broken and beaten bodies were strewn everywhere.

James lowered his weapon as a shiver ran through him. He had seen dead bodies before, but they were different. These people were just holidaymakers. They should be relaxing on the beach, not buried under piles of rubble. While James had not seen what happened, he had seen tsunami videos and could picture the carnage unfolding,

Behind him, something splashed. He spun around, his eyes falling on the pool. Moving forward, his rifle raised once more, James moved to the water's edge. Leaning over the pool, he stared into the murky water.

"Help me," a voice spoke, and a hand clamped on James's ankle.

He spun around, accidentally firing a burst from his M16 into the empty space behind the hotel. The shots rang out in the silent world. The hand on James's ankle jerked, causing him to lose his balance and fall into the pool.

The water was colder that he expected, the shock still resonating in the young corporal's mind. He took in a lungful of water. The slimy and brackish liquid flooded down his throat, moving like a living thing. James broke the surface, coughing and choking, the taste of the water making him retch.

James could stand in the pool, but in his panic, he flapped and swam for the side. He was hauling himself out when the half-eaten face turned his way.

"Help me," the voice repeated. One of the eyeballs hung from the socket, the ball sticking against the exposed raw meat of the cheek. The remainder of the face was covered in a layer of caked gore.

James screamed and dropped back into the water.

The figure pulled itself closer to the water, its hand stretching outwards. "In the water," it groaned.

James stared at it in horror. His mind replayed images of all the horror films he had seen over the years.

"Get away from me," he gasped.

"In the water."

James turned to swim to the other side of the pool.

"It's ... it's in the water," the voice called, shouting the final words.

James stopped swimming. Something in the man's cry chilled him to the bone. He started to turn, when something pulled his feet out from under him. Pain charged through his body, exploding out of him in a scream. His feet disappeared from under him and he sank beneath the surface, which grew cloudy with blood. Something thrashed against him, knocking the wind from his lungs, causing him to swallow another gulp of the slimy water.

Kicking out as hard as he could, James connected with something solid. The pressure on his leg disappeared, but pain intensified.

Pushing off the bottom of the pool, James tried to get back to his feet, but when he put his left leg down, he collapsed. Pain caused his vision to turn to black. He disappeared back beneath the water, his lungs burning. Something attacked him again, biting down onto his shoulder. His blood had turned the water into a reddish haze. He could not see own hands as they thrashed at whatever had clamped down onto his shoulder.

His hand latched onto something, but it pulled away, wrenching flesh from bone. James screamed as pain engulfed him. He grabbed hold of the pool siding and hauled himself free.

Blood spurted from his wounds, making the side of the pool slick. His grip slipped and he fell back. Catching himself, the young corporal heaved his shuddering body out of the water. He pulled himself clear and rolled over onto his back.

Breathing hard, he stared at the sky, his body trembled with shock. He could not move his injured arm; it hung dead and useless at his side. Forcing himself into a seated position, he looked at the pool and saw the creature that attacked him slipping beneath the surface. It looked like a large fish.

James followed the thick trail of blood, his blood, all the way to the bloody stump that had once been his foot.

His energy was spent. He couldn't move himself anymore. Sitting there, slumped against remains of a destroyed Tropicana-style bar, James Wyndham closed his eyes to rest.

***

Towards the south of the island, Anthony Henning heard the rattle of gunfire and spun around, expecting to find some terrorist cell closing in on him.

He had no idea what had happened on the island, but he knew that the tsunami that had swept through was not the beginning or the end of their troubles. He had seen dismembered body parts strewn along the path, along with the bodies of some of the strangest sea creatures he had ever seen, including one the size of a medium-sized dog. Its body stunk, already rotting under the blazing sun.

Henning believed in God. He believed in right and wrong, Heaven and Hell. He believed in his Lord and Saviour. He also believed that what had happened on the resort to be the work of evil. He had yet to see anybody left alive, while the body count powered into the double digits. He picked his way through the trees, those that remained standing were the least of his problems. Those pushed away by the power of the water created deep pools of water he needed to wade through and blockades that forced him to climb. Clothes and suitcases, dolls and teddy bears were caught in the rubble also, turning each one into a shrine to those that had died.

Anthony jumped down from the largest blockade yet and found himself on a stretch of beach. Large chunks of coral and

110

rocks stood half buried in the sand, as if he had walked into a giant aquarium. The only thing missing being a large skull or a pirate holding a 'no fishing' sign.

Moving forward, carefully stepping over the sand, Anthony worked his way through the coral. He gasped as he turned the corner and found a middle-aged man in a Speedo staring at him. The figure had been skewered in several places by the coral structure. The mouth hung open and a small crab dangled from the swollen purple tongue that barely fit in the man's mouth.

The smell of the ocean was heavy, and the strange coral graveyard did not serve to soothe the corporal's frayed nerves.

Behind him, the ocean lapped gently at the shore. Antony walked down to the surf, staring at the waves. He saw several bodies floating in the water, their bodies busy being reclaimed by the sea. He also saw something else a little further out, a shadow that moved under the water. He peered closer, but it was gone.

In the distance, Antony heard the thrum of the helicopter rotors starting up. He looked at his watch. He had to be getting back. Turning, he jogged out of the surf, missing the foot-long fish that leaped from the water, its jaws snapping at air.

The barbed lure that extended from under its jaws swiped at the air, tearing through the cloth of Anthony's trouser leg, missing the skin by a hair's breadth.

Anthony jogged through the trees, forced on by the knowledge that his ticket off the island and back to the DESRON unit was waiting for him.

He jumped from one of the tree dams, hurdling the pool that lay on the other side. He landed heavy, his ankle slipping in the mud. Anthony gave a yell and fell to the floor. He tried to roll, but his head hit a protruding tree stump, and his world went black.

When Anthony came too, his vision was a vague blur. His head pounded. He could feel the sticky warmth of blood on his face. He tried to move, but couldn't. His body did not feel his like his own. The commands he gave his floundering limbs did not reflect the actions that came.

Fumbling, Anthony brought his hand up to his face. He felt his jaw and the week of beard growth that covered it. He felt the blood, and further up found the source. He gave a cry, his body jerking as realization dawned on him. The pain that followed was intense.

The branch of the tree entered Anthony's skull through his eyeball and protruded out the back of his skull. It pinned him in place and made every movement excruciating. He tried reaching for his radio, but it was on his immobilised side.

Anthony had no idea how long he lay there, but his body grew cold and shuddered uncontrollably. He cried out when he heard the helicopter take off and pass by low overhead.

***

The sound of gunfire got Aiden moving. He put the strange creatures out of his mind and focused on getting to Melissa.

He didn't go very far before he caught sight of someone through the trees. Not more than a fleeting glimpse, but it gave him a direction. Moving fast, he cut through the remains of the forest, unaware that he was following the path that led directly to the dock.

He emerged from the trees and found the damage significantly reduced. Ahead of him was the long dock, what remained of it at least. The basic skeleton of the structure was still intact, but the large welcoming archway had collapsed, and blocked the docks entrance.

"Aiden?" a voice called out.

He spun around, looking for the voice's owner. "Melissa?" he called back, looking around.

"Up here. I can't believe you're here," Melissa called down.

Aiden looked up and saw his ex-wife. They stood a ways back, up on a ledge that looked down on the dock. He could see an easy path up to her, but before he could move, she broke into a run, heading towards him. Two men followed on her heels.

"Melissa, thank God you are alright." Aiden ran at his wife and pulled her into his arms. "What happened here? What are those things? We need to move. I have a chopper waiting to get us back to my DESRON unit. Where's Rachel? You can tell her it's safe, she can come out, we are getting out of here." Aiden spewed words as if racing the clock. His eyes never stopped roaming, looking for his daughter.

"Aiden, oh Aiden." Melissa started to cry.

"Mel, where is Rachel?" Aiden took hold of his wife by both shoulders.

"She's … she's dead."

CHAPTER 18

Aiden moved through a black abyss. He knew the direction and that people were following him, people he had rescued. Further than that, nothing mattered, or existed. He wanted to cry, to scream and rage. He wanted to break down and throw things. Grief overpowered his every sense, lost in the knowledge that his little girl was dead. What really tore his soul apart was the knowledge that there would be no body to bury, no piece of her to visit and mourn.

He tightened his grip on the rifle he held, and when they reached the pool where he first encountered the monstrous fish, he brought the weapon up before him and pulled the trigger. The bloated corpse of the freaky fish exploded in a shower of wet flesh.

"Easy, dude," Troy said, placing his hand on Aiden's shoulder. "We need to get off this fucking island, and we need you to hold it together long enough for that to happen. Now I'll take point, you hang back with Melissa, but I need to know which direction we need to move."

Aiden took his finger off the trigger, but the gunfire continued to echo around them. "The hotel. The chopper is waiting."

"Great, now let me take it from here." Troy assumed the lead and had them hurrying through what remained of the forest, towards the hotel.

They heard the thrum of the helicopter's motors before it came into view. The pilot stood waiting for them, his eyes nervously watching the treeline as they emerged. The relief on his face was palpable.

"Who are you?" the pilot asked as Troy ran up to the chopper. Behind him, Aiden appeared, and just behind them Raul and

Melissa came limping out of the trees, Raul all but carrying the distraught Melissa.

"No time to explain," Troy said, jumping into the back of the chopper. He jumped backwards and almost fell out when he saw the dead body lying opposite him. "What the hell?"

"Sorry, no time to explain," the pilot snarled. "Take a seat, we are airborne as soon as they get on board."

The pilot got behind the controls, and once he had Melissa and Raul safely in the back, Aiden jumped in, closed the door, and gave the signal to get into the air.

Melissa saw the body. It was still dripping wet, and the severed stump at the end of one leg still leaked blood like a slowly leaking tap. She stared at it and screamed, scratching and clawing at the chairs as she tried to put as much distance between her and it as possible.

"She's losing it. Do you have anything you can give her?" Troy asked up to Aiden, who sat looking much the worse for wear.

"What?" he asked, looking around.

"She needs a shot of something," Troy said again.

"Oh, sure, sure. Here." He handed a medical kit over the Troy. "There will be a shot of Diphenhydramine in there. That will calm her down until we get back to the ships." Aiden went through the motions, but his voice was still empty and emotionless.

Troy opened the pack, found the syringe, and after triple checking he had the right one, he took Melissa into his arms. She fell into him, the fight leaving her body, yet she remained rigid with panic. Troy gave her the shot and kissed her forehead. "I'm sorry," he whispered.

Troy looked up and saw Aiden staring at him. Something flashed in his eyes, but he turned his head away before Toy could get a fix on him.

"Where is Henning?" Aiden asked as they flew low over the island. He could make out the litany of bodies, both human and fish alike.

"He never made it back. I heard gunshots, but never saw him after you guys split," the pilot answered.

"Damn it," Aiden cursed. "Get us back to the ships. Something strange is happening here, and I want nothing to do with it."

Sitting in the chopper, the island and all his problems behind him, Troy realized how exhausted he was. It didn't take long before he fell into a semi-conscious doze. The next thing he remembered was the jolt as the bird landed back on the *USS Fitzgerald.*

CHAPTER 19

Captain Andrews stood waiting for them on the deck, clearly relieved to see his XO return unharmed, having received the reports of the casualties suffered.

He stood in silence as four of the crew carried Corporal Wyndham's body inside.

"What happened out there?" the captain asked his XO, but Aiden did not give an immediate answer. He stood with his ex-wife, hugging her, holding her tight.

Beside them, James Andrews recognized the figure of Troy Deane. "Good fight last time out, Mr. Dean. Maybe you could shed some light on things for me?"

"I think that is a discussion best kept for inside. The waters are not safe. We need to get further away from the island," Troy said. He knew he was speaking to the captain of the ship, but he couldn't care less.

All he wanted was to sit down, have a coffee, maybe a whiskey, and sleep. His body ached in a way he had not experienced in many years. Not since his five-round, non-title fight with Bruno Martinez. Martinez had been the champ at the time, and Troy stepped up on a week's notice. They went all five rounds, before the judges gave it to the champ on a split decision.

"I understand, of course, you must have been through a lot. Follow me." The captain turned and led the group inside.

Troy allowed Melissa and Aiden to go first. This time, he could not ignore the sneering look in Aiden's eyes as he walked by them.

"Jealousy is a horrid thing, especially in times of grief," Raul said, as he walked beside Troy.

"What do you mean?" Troy asked.

"I mean that there is more to their past than just a failed marriage. You two look good together, but that right there, that bond will be the elephant in the room," Raul whispered, not wanting to add any fuel to the fire he could see building.

They moved through the ship, through the twisting corridors, along the uniformed bodies of service men and woman on active duty.

"At least it isn't a submarine," Raul spoke as they entered the captain's cabin.

"Why, I thought you loved the water?" Troy said.

"I do, but not being cooped up on it," Raul answered.

"You two can freshen up in here. Sit and rest. There is some water and, just between us, something a little stronger in the cupboard by the bed there. I will come and fetch you for a debriefing later," the captain addressed Troy and Raul, before turning to lead Aiden and Melissa out into the ship.

"Aiden, take her to your cabin, and then meet me on the bridge. I want a full debriefing from you in ten minutes. I want to know how both men you took with you are now dead." Captain Andrews's voice was stern, but controlled. It commanded respect.

Aiden raised his head to look at his CO. "Sorry, sir. Yes, sir. Let me get her settled." Aiden wiped the tears from his eyes.

"Very good. By the way, where is your daughter, I didn't see her on the helo?" the captain asked without thinking, his mind going to the notion that she had not joined her mother for the holiday.

"She ... she didn't make it, sir." Aiden tried hard to choke back the tears

"Oh ... Oh Aiden, I'm so sorry. Debriefing can wait. Be with her now." James felt himself choking up at the thought of losing a child.

"Thank you, sir. One thing, if I can," Aiden asked, no longer trying to contain his grief.

"Anything."

"Get us as far away from that fucking island as you can."

"It's a promise, Lieutenant." James nodded his head and turned to move back to the bridge.

Aiden escorted Melissa into the XO's cabin and closed the door. The drugs Troy had given her were still in effect, and Melissa gave no resistance as Aiden lay her in his bed and covered her with the blanket.

Moving over to the desk, Aiden sat down, placed his head in his hands and started to weep. He reached over to the drawer and pulled out his wallet. He pulled out a crumpled picture of his daughter, a recent one, taken in the summer. She had sent it to him before their last deployment. Aiden found his hands trembling as he held it. Tears blurred his vision, and the fire of pain consumed him from within.

In the captain's cabin, Troy found himself unable to settle. He felt restless and paced the room. He did not like being locked up. The confines of the room did little to settle his nerves. He washed up and put his blood-encrusted clothes back on. He did not bring a change of clothes with him, and he doubted the captain would continue to be so hospitable if he decided to start wearing the man's reserve uniform.

"I need to go find her, make sure she is okay," Troy announced, walking towards the door.

"I wouldn't, man. I don't think we want to cause any trouble around here." Raul tried to talk Troy out of it, but knew the look of a stubborn man when he saw one.

"They are not together. He wasn't there with her when this happened. I was, I saw that little girl in the water. I need to be with her." Troy knew his emotions had gotten the better of him, but he figured he had earned the right to let them dictate things for a while.

"It's your funeral, buddy," Raul said with a smile.

Leaving the room, Troy found himself momentarily lost on the inside of the destroyer, but he soon caught his bearings and made a best guestimate as where he would find Melissa. He knocked on the door to the XO's cabin and waited. He could not hear anything on the inside. The general humdrum of the ships operations drowned out such fine hearing.

He raised his bandaged hand to knock again, when the door opened. Aiden looked at him, his eyes red with sorrow.

"What?"

"Hi, I was just wondering how Melissa is. Can I come in?" Troy asked.

"No, she needs to be with family. Besides, she's resting," Aiden snarled.

"Well, I think she would want me to be there with her." Troy felt a sure of energy rush through him.

"I don't think you know what she wants. Who the hell are you to say what she wants? Some juiced-up wreck who doesn't know when to retire." His words were vicious, and laced with an agony Troy could not understand.

"Hey, hey, hold on there, buddy. I know you both lost someone today. I get that, but you are not married anymore. She and I, well, well, we are figuring out what we are, but I know Melissa would want to have me there with her, when she wakes up." Troy knew he should be more tactful, but he had been through just as much as anybody else on the island. He did not like the idea of some sailor playing macho man at his expense. He refused to just bend over and take it.

"Fuck you, get back to the room before I have them lock you away," Aiden spat.

"Aiden, Aiden?" Melissa's voice came from inside the room.

"I believe that's my name she is calling. Thank you for coming around. Now go away." Aiden slammed the door to his cabin and left Troy standing along in the hallway.

Troy clenched his fists, wincing against the pain, but consumed by rage. He did not like Melissa's ex-husband, and under any other circumstances, he would have knocked him out by that point of a discussion.

Rather than head back to the cabin, where he knew his emotions would only stew, instead Troy followed the hallway in search of the bridge. He knew he looked a state, but he needed to make sure the captain understood the dangers. He knew Aiden had seen the fish, but he had not seen the monster that rose with the tsunami. He had not seen it sink a ferry boat with ease.

The captain needed to know what was out there, and prepare themselves to fight if needed.

***

"Who was that?" Melissa asked, groggy from the sedative.

"That, oh, nobody. Just one of the seamen bringing us some towels to clean up," Aiden lied.

"Oh, I thought it might have been Troy," she said, the hurt heavy in her voice.

"Nope, he hasn't been here." Aiden felt bad at lying, but he didn't want Troy around his ex-wife. He didn't want any man around her, not in that way. "You need to rest. Stay here, while I go talk to the captain."

"Aiden."

"Yes."

"You need to tell him, there is something in the water," Melissa began.

"The fish, I know. I saw them." Aiden smoothed Melissa's hair and made her lie back in the bed.

"No," she said sitting back up. "Something else. Something even larger. It's a beast. It took out the ferry. I mean it, this creature was the size of a whale, bigger."

"It's okay. You are safe now. You survived a disaster, everything will be fine," Aiden soothed, ignoring the warning Melissa tried to give.

"You don't understand. Speak to Troy, and Raul," Melissa pleaded, drifting back off to sleep before she realized Aiden had already left.

The bridge buzzed with activity, as the DESRON unit swung themselves around to head back home. The *Fitzgerald* was one of the newer ships in the unit, along with the *USS Brown, Rosamilia,* and *Woodhead.* The *Brown* help the honour of being the lead ship, under the power of Captain Christopher Abbott. He was a younger man, pushed through the ranks and positions in near record time. Many considered him to be a leader of the new age. He was liked by all but the more senior serving captains, who saw his ways as sloppy and lackadaisical.

Captain Andrews liked Abbott. He had not given him a hard time about sending the chopper to rescue Aiden's family. Even so, he dreaded having to explain how two men died during said rescue mission. He had held off making the call himself and had ignored two incoming calls from the COMDESRON. He knew he could not wait much longer and not risk disciplinary action.

"Captain, there is someone here that wants to talk to you," one of the officers on watch said, motioning across the bridge to where a bloodied and bruised Troy stood waiting.

"Very good, show him in, Mr. McAffrey," Captain Andrews said, nodding with a large enough movement for Troy to understand his request for an audience with the captain had been granted.

"What can I do for you, Mr. Dean?" the old officer asked.

"You know me," Troy said, his usual reaction when people recognized him. After all the years of being a fighter, the fact that people knew his face continually caught Troy off guard.

"Well, we don't get a lot of TV options, and cage fighting is a popular sport throughout the forces," James answered.

"I'm beginning to get a picture of things. I've only been on board an hour or so and I feel as if I'm coming down with cabin fever." Troy smiled, hoping the captain took it as a joke and not an insult.

"Yeah, you get used to it pretty fast though. This ship is a family. A unit. We watch each other's backs. You got brothers, Mr. Deane?" James asked.

"No, no sir, I don't, and please, call me Troy." Troy offered his hand, unsure of the proper etiquette when addressing a ship's captain.

"James Andrews, Captain of the USS Fitzgerald. We didn't plan on having any visitors, so our entertainment options are rather limited. I might be able to get you a cup of decent coffee, if you are happy for it to be strong enough to clean your car engine, and maybe just a little bit lumpy."

"Lumpy is fine with me, as long as it is hot and wet." Troy smiled.

"Aha, a man after my own heart." Captain Andrews smiled. "I like my coffee like I like my women."

"How's that, sir?" Troy asked, setting up the punchline for the old man.

"Black or white, it doesn't matter as long as she is bitter." The older man burst out and laughing, a guffawed belly laugh. Troy laughed too. He had not heard that variant of the line before.

"But I'm not here to talk about coffee, sir. I want to tell you about the resort. The island. There is something you don't understand. There are —"

"Captain, we have something on sonar," a voice interrupted them.

"Excuse me, Mr. Deane," Captain Andrews apologized, as he walked away.

Troy followed out of pure curiosity. He couldn't believe it was the creature from the island. Why would it attack them?

"Captain, we've got a huge school of fish coming this way. Moving fast, too," the sonar operator spoke, his face glued to the screens.

"Son, do we look like a fishing trawler?" Captain Andrews asked.

"No, sir."

"You have come across fish before, right? Either before or during your time in the Navy?" Captain Andrews continued.

"Yes, sir," the technician answered.

"Good. We are a DESRON unit, we are not concerned by schools of fish." Captain Andrews clapped the young officer on the shoulder and turned to find Troy standing right behind him.

"Mr. Deane, if there is nothing else I can do for you, I will have the coffee sent to my cabin," Captain Andrews spoke politely, but made it clear that Troy's time on the bridge had reached its end.

"I'm sorry, Captain, but I couldn't help but overhear. Those fish. I think, I think they could be a real problem. You see, to cut a long story short, fish destroyed the resort back there. They killed everybody, and there are a lot more of them in the water." Troy knew how crazy it sounded, but he knew the truth, and in his head, that simply outranked everything else.

"Mr. Dean, Troy, you said, right?" Troy nodded. "You have been through a lot. We had reports of a tsunami in the area. That is what damaged the resort. An underwater earthquake. I am sure there were lots of fish around the island, and a great many caught in that tidal rush, but please, do not take me for a fool."

Troy took a slow deep breath. "I have no intention of doing that, Captain. You have to listen to me. Ask the others, they will confirm it too. Those fish came up with the quake. They were set free from some deep-earth prison. They are not like normal fish." Troy raised his voice a little and stood square to the captain. He made use of his three-inch height advantage and his much wider upper body, making himself as large as possible as he spoke.

"I will not be spoken to like that —"

"Captain, it's the *Woodhead,* they are under attack," the communications officer called out, interrupting the pair.

Captain Andrews turned and strode across the bridge followed by Troy. "Get me Captain Davenport," Captain Andrews ordered.

"Already have him, sir," the man answered promptly.

"Woodhead, this is Captain Andrews of the *Fitzgerald,* what's going on out there?" For a few moments, they heard nothing but the rumble of static.

"James, it's Riley, we are under attack, fish, large fish. They have already breached our hull. We're taking on water in the bow," Riley Davenport, Captain of the US *Woodhead,* answered.

The two captains had known each other for many years, yet their assignments to the DESRON were their first within the same unit.

"Fish, as you sure?" Captain Andrews asked.

"Sure as snow in winter," Captain Davenport replied. "They attacked us in a swarm. We never even saw them coming. Well, we did, but, I mean, they were fish."

For a few moments, Captain Andrews found himself speechless. He stared at Troy, open mouthed.

"Where are they now?" he asked.

"They pulled back. We have them on sonar, but they are deep. They came up, attacked us, and dropped back down again," Captain Davenport answered.

"How badly damaged are you?"

"We are still moving. Limping a bit, but nothing that will slow us down too much. All free hands are busy on it," Riley answered. "Keep your eyes open, James. I have no idea what those things are, but they can do some serious damage, and they have numbers on their side."

"Captain, we have incoming targets," the sonar technician called out.

"Direction?" Captain Andrews moved swiftly through the bridge, as suddenly everything changed. The atmosphere became serious with such swiftness that Troy could feel the change as if it were a brisk wind rising up on a calm day.

"Coming from the southwest. Moving at forty knots, they should be here in under five minutes." Concern weighed heavily on every word the technician spoke.

"Forty knots?"

"Yes, sir. That school of fish sped up. It looks like they are attacking us," the technician said, looking up at his CO.

"Man the .50 calibres, I want lead flying as soon as they come into range. Get the CIWS online too, but hold off on firing until my signal," Captain Andrew's ordered. "Get me Captain Abbott, he needs to know what is going on."

The bridge became a flurry of activity; everybody had a job to do, and they carried it out efficiently. To Troy, it looked like organized chaos.

"Mr. Dean, come with me," the captain called.

Troy followed as they left the bridge and hurried down to the captain's ready room, which was the same size as the captain's cabin and connected by an internal door. The phone connected to the *Brown,* where Captain Christopher Abbott already waited for them.

"What's going on? The *Woodhead* is injured and I see you just brought your weapons systems online," Captain Abbott asked. While he had risen rapidly through the ranks, it could not be denied that certain political elements had also contributed to his stellar career. The other captains in the DESRON unit were battle tested.

"Yes, sir, the same things that attacked the resort are attacking us." Captain Andrews chose his words carefully, but Abbott was no fool.

"What sort of creatures? What on this earth would attack a US destroyer?" the inevitable question came.

"Fish, they are fish." Silence from the other end of the line. "Captain Abbott, we have someone on board who can shed some light on things, but you need to take this threat seriously, however crazy it sounds."

"I believe you, James. Do what is necessary, and I will inform the other captains, and the folks back home."

"Yes, sir. Stay safe, Captain." The exchange ended, and Captain Andrews set off immediately. The man had not stopped since Troy first met him.

Troy followed obediently, the time and need for cordial invitations had passed.

The bridge had settled down, but the overtones of seriousness were clear. Everybody was focused. Nobody spoke unless they needed to. The chatter and banter had died. Things had gotten real.

"I need an update," the captain announced as he walked.

"Sir, they dropped down deeper. Our guns can't touch them," the weapons officer replied.

"Shit, are they still heading this way?" A sense of urgency crept into the captain's voice.

"No, sir, actually they are not. They have changed course," the sonar technician replied.

"Well, don't keep us in suspense, man. Where are they heading?" Captain Andrews prompted.

"They are heading for the *Woodhead*, sir." The technician swallowed hard. "Closing at over forty knots, Captain."

Captain Andrews stormed over the bridge, moving at close to a run. "Raise the *Woodhead*."

"Captain, the *Woodhead* has fired torpedoes. We have two fish in the water."

"Bring it up on screen," Captain Andrews roared.

Troy stood in the middle of the bridge, caught up in the moment. Not sure where he should stand; to follow the captain, or to anticipate his next move.

The large screen, which until that minute had been a see through panel in front of the wall, changed to show a shot from a camera mounted on the exterior of the ship. Troy could see the white streaks where the torpedoes sped beneath the surface.

"What is he doing on the bridge?" Aiden's voice cut through the pre-combat humdrum.

"Lieutenant, good to have you back. We have contact with a school of unsubs," Captain Andrews spoke.

"Not this fish crap again. Sir, the fish I saw on the island were ugly as sin, but would not be a threat to us." Aiden moved beside his CO, snarling towards Troy.

"Tell that to the *Woodhead,* Lieutenant." Captain Andrews did not take his eyes off the monitor as he spoke.

"Contact, sir," a voice called just as a plume of water, steam, and fish guts rose into the air.

"Reports, did they get them?" the captain asked, eager.

"Negative, sir. The blast took out a number of the fish, but the school is still charging on the ship. Impact in less than thirty seconds," another voice called.

To Troy, the voices were indistinguishable from the people surrounding him. He could not tell who spoke and when. Everybody stared at their station, not looking up to talk, but taking their turn when necessary.

"God help them. They are on their own for the time being. Bring the ship around, I want to be ready to move in if needed," the captain gave the order and turned to address Troy, and Aiden, who stood beside him.

They watched the shadow grow beneath the water, as the school rose. The dark mass spread like oil, until it was far larger than the ship they were attacking.

The *Woodhead* shook and rocked on the water as the surface broke as if boiling. The fish threw their bodies at the destroyer, battering the hull. On the deck, the guns began to fire, strafing the water with hot .50 calibre lead. The water turned red, but the onslaught continued.

He destroyer listed heavily by the time the attack stopped. Its lower levels were flooded. The *Woodhead* was sinking.

"What the hell did we just see?" Aiden asked.

"You saw those what those fish did to your destroyer. Next time, maybe you won't be such an asshole when I try and give you a warning," Troy snarled at Aiden.

"What the fuck did you say?" Aiden spun around and shoved Troy backwards.

"You heard me. You're pissed with me. I get it. I fucked your wife, wait, she's your ex, right? Geez, I guess it doesn't concern you after all." Troy stepped forward until he stood nose-to-nose with Aiden.

"Get off this bridge, before I throw you off this boat," Aiden snarled.

"Make me," Troy couldn't help himself say.

"Lieutenant Quinn, stand down this instant," Captain Andrew's whispered, so as not to draw any more attention to the incident. "You have been through a lot, so I will let that slide, but I will not have it happen again. Do I make myself clear?"

"Yes, sir," Aiden replied, never once breaking his gaze with Troy.

"I want the choppers in the air; we need to lay down some fire and buy them some time. I want us to take as many officers off the *Woodhead* as possible, lighten them up." The captain turned his back on the two men and resumed his duties running the ship.

"You heard the man," Troy said with a smirk plastered on his face. "Run along, little doggy."

"This isn't over. I don't care who you are. Melissa will see through this summer fling, trust me." Aiden's face flushed with anger.

"You're just jealous that I got her and you lost her," Troy laughed and walked away.

CHAPTER 20

Riley Davenport braced for the impact. Their torpedoes had done nothing but scratch the surface of the body of fish.

They battered the hull with enough force that the echoes of their impact to resonated through the entire ship. It sounded like they were stuck in a caravan during a hail storm.

Alarms began to ring on the bridge, different consoles all reporting back different damage statuses. On the deck, the guns were blazing, firing into the water blind. The attack seemed never ending, yet fell away in an instant. The fish disappeared, driving themselves back down deep beneath the ship.

"I need damage reports, ASAP," Captain Davenport roared. He could already feel the boat beginning to list.

"We are taking on water, sir. Multiple breaches in the hull. I don't know what those things are, but they hit hard," a voice spoke up from behind a whirring console.

"Do we still have power in the engines?" Riley asked, forcing himself to keep his voice calm.

"Yes, sir. We are limping a little, but we are far from dead in the water," the response came from the engine room.

"We are taking on water, but I think we should have enough time left to limp ourselves home," another report came back.

"Good. I want two more fish in the tubes, ready to fire again if they make a second attack. Keep the guns ready, get the R2 unit online. Those motherfuckers make another move, we will hit them with everything we've got." It felt utterly insane that they were talking in such a way. "I'll be damned if we lose this boat to some fucking fish."

Below the bridge, on the lower levels of the boat, engineers were busy trying to report the damage, seal up the leaks and pump out as much water as they could.

Randy Dalgliesh was one such man. Limping into the final years of his career, he was an old man whose body was filled with aches and pains of sea life. Not tied down to the same terms of service as the officers above him, many found him too old to still be at sea. They were right, but Randy did not know any other way of life, and had no desire to learn about them now.

He heaved his equipment into place and looked around. The water reached ankle deep. He identified three holes in the hull that needed to be patched. Crouching down to start, he pulled the visor over his eyes and fired up the acetylene torch.

He worked quickly and had the first hole patched up in no time. His knees cried out as he stood back up, but he pushed on. Grabbing another place, he moved to the second hole. Behind him, something splashed in the water. Randy spun around, unusually jumped given the circumstances.

"Hello?" he called. He felt stupid when no answer came.

He turned back to the task at hand when something brushed against him. He looked down and saw something moving through the water. It swam so fast he could not get a look at it.

"A fucking fish. Great," he muttered.

Bending down to get back to work, Randy became aware that the fish had circled around him. It struck fast. Leaping from the water to his right, he turned to swat it away when the teeth clamped down. They crushed through bone and severed his wrist with a quick wrench of the powerful body.

Randy screamed and fell back into the water. His torch fell and died with an angry hiss. Clutching his bloodied stump, Randy screamed. He tried to move backwards in the water, but couldn't find any grip.

"Jesus, ah, God," he cried, letting go of his injured hand to fumble for the radio.

Two more fish appeared, their thick bodies barely contained by the shallow water. They gained on him, rising as they did. Moving like sharks, coming in for the kill. Randy kicked out with the toe of his boot and caught one of the fish in the body. The fish bit down, teeth slicing through the steel toecaps and into the flesh below. Blood squirted into the air like an oil strike.

Randy fell backwards, struggling to break free. The third fish tore his face from his skull, cutting the cranium in half in the process.

The door stood open, and water gushed into the hallway, pulling the fish along with it. The three spilled into the belly of the ship, their semi-submerged bodies powered on by strong fins and a fighting spirit.

On the bridge, Riley Davenport prepared to fight. His choppers were locked, loaded, and ready to take to the skies.

"Sir, we have another target moving in," his sonar technician called.

"Is it the fish?" he asked.

"Negative. This is a solid mass, and ... and it's huge," the technician answered, his voice shaking as he spoke.

"How large?" Riley asked.

"The same size as us, sir."

"Give me a location, bring it up on screen," Riley ordered, moving over to the captain's chair. The screen appeared, and in the distance, he could make out the shadow beneath the surface of the water.

"It will be on us in four minutes, sir. Moving at thirty-seven knots," the sonar tech called out.

"Is it a submarine?"

"Negative, it is organic, sir."

"That's impossible. Only a whale could be that size, and they don't move that fast," Riley replied, thinking out loud. "Get us moving, I don't care what it takes. I need as much power out of those engines as I can get."

"Captain, three minutes out, speed has increased to forty knots," the sonar tech called, near screamed.

"How are we looking on the torpedoes?" Riley called through to the weapons officer.

"The rear tubes are damaged, but we still have two good tubes locked and loaded up front, Captain." The voice that answered was strained, and not that of the weapons officer.

"Then fire two. I want fish in the water now." The order was met with silence, but a few moments later, the ship shuddered as the two warheads were ejected into the water.

"Two minutes, captain."

"Brace yourselves, these two are going to meet somewhere in the middle," Riley called.

Silence fell for a moment, while all eyes focused on the screen.

"Sir, the target has dropped deeper. It's passed under the fish."

"Under them?"

"Yes sir, they made the turn, but … brace for impact, sir." The warning came a few moments too late. The target hit the *Woodhead* with the force of a large detonation. It tore through the metal, like a burrowing worm. The fish passed through the ship before leaving the other side. The large hole left behind sent water pouring into the *Woodhead*, condemning her to her fate.

The force of the explosion shook the entire vessel and sent everybody from the bridge down flying. The screams of those on the lower levels echoed through the stricken vessel, only to be silenced by the rampaging water that tore through the hollow innards like blood surging through arteries.

Riley Davenport knew it was too late the moment it happened. He tried to move from the floor, but his legs would not respond. His spine had snapped from the jarring impact he had with the computer console behind him.

The cries of his crew echoed around in an eerie wail. They were soon silenced by the impact of the two torpedoes. The warheads hit the ship either side of the damaged hull.

A tower of flames consumed the *Woodhead*, and within minutes, the burning sections were swallowed by the sea.

CHAPTER 21

The crew of the *Fitzgerald* watched in silence as the flames subsided and the blank space that had once held the *Woodhead* came into view.

"What the hell?" Nobody knew who spoke. They were all stunned in disbelief.

"Sir, target is coming around again. It's heading for us," the sonar tech yelled.

"Fire torpedoes," Captain Andrews reacted.

The boat shuddered, as if a chill had been sent down its hull.

"Torpedoes are in the water, sir," a voice came over the transmission from deeper in the ship.

Captain Andrews turned toward Troy. Tension etched into his face, from the clenched jaw to the steel-set eyes. "You said someone else could explain more?" he said, swallowing down his emotions.

"Yeah, Raul, he's sitting in your cabin. I'm not saying he knows what is going on but —"

"I can give you some answers," Raul interrupted, making the three men in the centre of the discussion jump.

"Jesus wept, don't we have any security on this bridge?" Captain Andrews roared. "Tell me everything you know and make it fast."

An explosion rocked the ocean as the torpedoes found their mark. The ocean swelled as the warheads detonated deep beneath the surface.

"We have a direct hit. The sonar is clear," the voice announced.

"We killed it?" Captain Andrews pushed for confirmation.

"I can't confirm it sir, but everything seems clear ... no ... I have something. It's further out. It's running away."

"What about the others?"

"They seem to be moving with it, sir."

"Turn this ship around. They started this fight, but we will damned well be the ones to finish it. It's going to pay for what it did to the *Woodhead*," Captain Andrews snarled, standing defiant in the centre of the bridge.

"Captain, what about the rest of the DESRON?" Aiden asked, stepping forward, out of the haze that held him.

"They will follow us. I spoke with Captain Abbott and he approved all action necessary," he answered.

The remaining destroyers made a wide circle and headed back out to see, following the large fish out into deeper, cooler water. The *Fitzgerald* pushed itself to the limit, speeding after its target, while the *Rosamilia* followed behind at a slower speed, with the *Brown* purposefully holding back.

As the flagship of the DESRON, it was her duty to oversee manoeuvers. They would act as a sweeper should either the fish or the school cut back out and around. Not that anybody believed the creatures were intelligent enough to ponder military strategy, but with the *Woodhead* gone, no chances were being taken.

Captain Andrews placed his hand on Raul's shoulder and led him away, the pair already locked deep in conversation, leaving Aiden in control of the bridge. He had his game face on and paid no mind to Troy, who took the opportunity to disappear and head in search of Melissa.

He left the bridge without so much as a question being thrown his way. Moving without thinking, Troy found himself standing outside of the XO's cabin. His hand shook when he went to knock. What if Aiden had been telling the truth? What if she didn't want to see him? She could blame him for Rachel's death, after all; if they had not been together, who knows if Rachel would have even gone to the lake. A myriad of thoughts surged through Troy's head, swirling around like a hurricane.

Troy closed his eyes, focused, and knocked. When nobody answered, he turned to leave when the door opened and Melissa peered through the crack. Her eyes took him in, studying him for a second, before she opened the door.

"Where were you?" she asked. Her eyes were red from crying.

"I came, but your Prince Charming would not let me in," Troy spat, too tired, and too old to mince his words.

"What?" Melissa asked, sluggish.

"Aiden, I came to see you but he wouldn't let me in. He said you didn't want to see me. Given that this is kind of his house, I couldn't just force my way in. Trust me, I tried, and I wanted to see you." Troy felt his body shake and heard his voice quiver.

A moment later and they were in each other's arms, not lost to the throes of passion, but rather the more gratifying sensation of having a companion, a soulmate that helps to fight against the pain, the sadness, and the anger that comes with life.

"I'm glad you came back. Are we almost home? I have no idea what's going on. What happened to me?" Melissa asked, scratching at her head.

"Well, there has been a slight change of plan. Those fish attacked the boats. They sank one, and now we are chasing them down," Troy explained, decided that the Band-Aid approach was probably going to be the best for all concerned.

"What?"

"Trust me, this is still the safest place to be. The wounded them, the big fish. They hurt it, and now they are going to finish the job." Troy didn't know who he was trying to convince with such a speech, but it seemed to work.

Back on the bridge, Aiden ordered the ships engines increased to full thrust. They were already redlining before he issued the command for more. The fish moved fast through the water, and he would not let them get away. He stood with his fists clenched, his blood still boiling at the way Troy strutted around the ship like he owned it.

Looking about, he realized that the man had disappeared, and had to catch the angry growl that grew from his throat.

To his left, his CO was lost in conversation with another one of the men he had rescued. None of it sat well with Aiden, who felt as if he were being forced out of something that he had technically started. It had been his wish to rescue his wife and daughter. He didn't plan on bringing a team onto the boat and have them start calling all the shots.

His fists were clenched so tight they began to ache. He opened his hands and shook them, trying to loosen them but, but the rage was too deep-seated for it to work.

"So tell me, what do you know about those fish?" Captain Andrews asked Raul.

He had led the man across the bridge, affording them what privacy he could

"I don't know much. I think I know where they came from, and what caused it, but I'm not saying there is much more behind it than plain guesswork," Raul answered. He had spent enough time aboard military vessels, and he had no interest in playing games economizing the truth, just for the sake of being able to claim the bigger dick.

"I don't care. Right now, we know nothing about these sons of bitches, other than that they attack with ferocity and don't seem to care what happens," the captain answered.

"They are old, older than we can imagine. I think when they build that resort island, they woke them up. Cracked open their pen, and set them free. They came from deep underground. They are ancient, and stronger than we could know. They will attack because they see us as a threat. I would even suggest that during their time in the world, they were the biggest predator, the fiercest in any case. They are attacking us because we pose a threat to them," Raul spoke slowly, not wanting to give the impression he knew more than he already divulged.

"What are they?" Captain Andrews asked.

"I don't know. I mean, they look like dragonfish, the deep sea kind, but they are only half a foot long, and live around five thousand feet below. You have different levels of the ocean. The fish are attaching at the top level. We call it Epipelagic Zone, or the Sunlight Zone. These things live two zones deeper in the Bathypelagic Zone, or the Midnight Zone. They are nasty-looking things, and tough as nails to survive and thrive down at that depth. Creatures this size, they could do some serious damage," Raul said.

"That is why we are going to stop them," Captain Andrews answered with conviction. "The question is, are there any more of them out there?"

Raul did not answer straight away. Not because he didn't know the answer, but because he needed to make sure the answer he gave did not get turned against him. "I don't think so. They came from deep down, and the quakes brought them to the surface. It's all because of the island. Who knows what else could be down there. From a scientific perspective, it is fascinating. I mean, these creatures could change the seas of this planet forever. They would be the ultimate predator."

"You sound excited by that idea." The captain regarded Raul with a curious eye.

"I am a scientist, sir. It is fascinating. I walked away from the profession, but my love for it never died. These creatures need to be stopped, I can agree to that, but it does not stop my brain from wondering." Raul smiled, hoping he had not lost any standing in the captain's opinion.

He stopped caring about other people's opinions many years before, but while a guest on the military boat, he wanted to make sure he remained in place to get a good view of proceedings, and not be resigned to some windowless cabin.

"I appreciate that. I respect it. We will see what a fearful predator it is when we unload the wrath of good ole Lady Liberty on it." The captain smiled and returned his attention to the bridge. "That will be all for now, Lieutenant. Why don't you take a break, grab some coffee and freshen up, I have control of things here."

"Thank you, sir. I believe I will," Aiden answered, keen to leave the bridge. He just knew he would find Troy in his cabin, and it incensed him more with each passing second.

Aiden stormed from the bridge and down the stairwell to his cabin, all but pushing two younger seamen over as he barged between them. One man began to say something, until he noticed Aiden's uniform and fell silent.

Pulling open the door to his cabin, Aiden charged in, his mind prepared to find Melissa and Troy going at it like a couple of drunk college students. What he found only enraged him further.

They were sitting on the bed, Melissa leaning against Troy. His arm wrapped around her, holding her tight while she wept.

"Get out of this cabin. You do not have authority to be in here," Aiden thundered, unable to control himself. His emotions were all over the place, and in that moment, they took control, and started calling the shots.

"Aiden," Melissa gasped, wiping her eyes.

"You heard me, get out," he spat, his eyes burning daggers into Troy.

"Not going to happen, buddy," Troy refused, holding Melissa even tighter. "Unless Melissa wants me to leave."

"No, stay. Aiden, he stays. I need him here," Melissa stammered.

"No, you don't. You need me, you need your family. Not some holiday boy toy," Aiden snarled. Striding forward, he grabbed Troy by the shirt and hauled him to his feet. "Now I said, get out."

Aiden tried to manhandle Troy towards the door, but the fighter resisted with ease. He slipped from Aiden's grasp and turned around to face him.

"Just calm down. You have been through a lot, I get that," Troy said, ducking out of the way just as Aiden through a big haymaker punch.

"Aiden, stop it," Melissa screamed, rising up from the bed.

Aiden swung again, another blow that Troy easily dodged.

"Come on, man, I'm not going to fight you," Troy said, ducking a third, erratic swing.

"Fuck you," Aiden roared, throwing the chair across the room to clear a path towards Troy.

Melissa moved forward and grabbed his hand. "Aiden, stop this," she cried.

Aiden didn't hear her, rage consumed him. He swatted her away without hesitation. Melissa fell to the floor, stumbling over the chair Aiden had thrown. She landed badly on the floor.

"Melissa," Troy called, leaping into action. He lowered his shoulder, drove it into Aiden's midsection. Wrapping his arms around the winded soldier's body, he picked him with a grunt of exertion. Their bodies twisted, and Troy slammed Aiden down onto the table. He followed it up with two heavy shots to Aiden's unguarded face.

As he prepared to throw another succession of blows, Melissa's voice reached out to him. She urged him to stop. The pain in her words made his rage fall away. He released his grip on Aiden's shirt and stood up. Aiden rolled from the table, fighting to stay conscious; he fell to the floor, landing in a groaning heap.

Silence filled the cabin. Troy looked from Melissa to Aiden and back again. He felt guilty, but the man had pushed him.

"Troy," Melissa began, her voice soft. "Can you leave us, please?"

Troy went to say something, but Melissa's gaze held the words in his throat.

"It's okay, I promise." She smiled and bent down to tend to Aiden.

Troy's fists had made short work of his face. His nose was broken and both eyes were closed behind an ugly mass of swollen, discoloured flesh. Troy didn't say anything, but turned and left the room. He returned to the bridge, simply because he had nowhere else to go.

"What happened?" Captain Andrews asked, when he saw the blood on Troy's shirt.

"Nothing, sir," Troy lied.

"Okay, well, I hope nothing else is not going to happen," the old captain said.

"No, sir."

It had gotten dark outside; the stars were out and gave some illumination, but out at sea, the darkness became total. The ocean and the sky combined, the horizon ceased to exist. Troy found it a very disorienting experience.

"Captain, I have the targets. They are on the edge of the screen, but they have slowed down. I think they are turning around," the sonar tech reported.

"Focus on the big one. I want that son of a bitch dead." Captain Andrews stood tall in the middle of the bridge, his eyes set on the darkness. "Prepare the torpedoes, fire on my order," he spoke

With the ship ready for battle, Troy found the close quarters growing even tighter. The walls seemed that much closer, the air suddenly tasted stuffy and stale. He had not noticed it before, but every breath left an old, oily taste in his mouth.

"Sir, both targets are gaining on it. Closing in from the north, moving at close to forty knots." A quiet murmur filled the bridge.

"Fire the torpedoes," the order went up, and a few moments later, the fish were in the water and speeding away from the ship.

"Look," Troy called out, pointing through the bridge's window. The white streams of the two warheads gave a little more perspective to the nightscape. Ahead of them, the water took on a strange blue glow. "What is that?"

"That's them. The fish," Raul answered. "Dragonfish have a phosphorous zone on the back of their heads. It glows blue, especially when they are hunting or mating."

"What do you think they are doing now?" Troy asked, feeling stupid the moment he heard the question.

"I hope they are hunting us, because I sure as hell don't want to mate with that big motherfucker," Raul answered deadpan, but shot Troy a wink when he caught the fighter looking his way. "We are a threat to them. They are the top dog. They thing they can hunt the torpedoes. I almost feel sorry for the stupid bastards."

"Yeah, almost," Troy answered quietly.

"Sir, the *Rosamilia* has fired torpedoes also. Heading to the west. The school is attacking. It's … it's like they are trying to flank us. The *Brown* is also reporting incoming targets from the west," a frantic voice spoke up. Troy had long since given up on trying to decipher who had spoken.

"God damn it. They think they are smart, do they? I want the stern tubes loaded. Send out a volley of CAPTORs and see how they like them eggs." Captain Andrews moved through the bridge, checking screens and watching from all angles.

Troy watched and then something dawned on him. The captain was in the zone. Troy would recognize that look anywhere.

The ship rocked again as more torpedoes were launched. The first explosion rocked the invisible skyline. The plume of water billowed into the air, and glistened with blue flakes.

"Sir, we have a direct hit." A round of applause ran through the bridge, and a few minutes later, the second torpedo struck its target. More blue flakes littered the night air, floating around like fireflies.

The round of applause increased, as whoops and whistles were thrown into the mix. Even Captain Andrews clapped his hands together

"I'll need confirmation," he said to the technician.

"The target appears to have been destroyed, sir, but the big one is still out there. The school broke off into two. It's like they tried to trick us. The other creature is still out there," the technician replied, his words being cut off by the sound of repeated explosions.

"Sir, the CAPTOR mines deployed, but I still have a target. It is moving in on the *Rosamilia,*" a worried voice spoke from behind a second sonar console

"Fire torpedoes," Captain Andrews replied without hesitation.

"We can't, sir. The creature is too close to the *Rosamilia*," the technician answered.

"Balls," Captain Andrews growled, slamming his fist onto the top of the computer console.

The crew of the *Rosamilia* were helpless. They had released a volley of torpedoes at the school of fish coming at them, and had not seen the larger creature until it broke away from the group, coming at them from the side. The creature had gone through the CAPTOR mines without flinching.

The force of their explosions slowed it down, but did not halt its progress. The fish hit the destroyer close to the front, shearing away the forward compartments, caving in the iron as if it were an aluminium can.

This impact was swiftly followed by the third Mk-46 torpedo released by the CAPTOR mines laid by the *Fitzgerald.* The explosion hit the loaded forward tubes and set off a secondary round of explosions that saw fire go barrelling through the corridors like blood through veins.

The screams of the men were brief, as the fireball silence them before the true agony of their deaths could be realized. The

Rosamilia sank before anybody had a chance to understand what had truly happened.

"Lay down fire. Get those .50 calibres spitting lead, now," Captain Robert Nash ordered. He stood tall, his hand held to his head, keeping pressure on the deep wound that stretched several inches over his forehead and onto his scalp. Blood blinded one eye, but he would not roll over without a fight.

"Sir, the CIWS is offline," a groggy voice shouted.

"Then load the torpedoes and fire," Nash bellowed, stumbling through the bridge. The initial shot from the creature had sent them all flying. The explosions that came as result and sent them sprawling. Three of Nash's highest ranking officers were lying dead on the floor, their necks twisted at an odd angle, their blood-stained faces forever frozen into a look of pain.

"Sir, the creature is closing fast, it's too close," the man began to contradict.

"Fire the fucking torpedoes. If we are going to Hell, then they son of a bitch is going with us," Nash roared.

"Aye, Captain," the response came. Silence fell as it seemed the entire ship, or those that remained alive at least, caught wind of the captain's plan. Their time was up, and they knew it.

The ship shuddered. The torpedoes were launched and collided with the charging fish. The explosion tore a hole in the side of the ship and water rushed in, charging to meet the still-burning inferno in the lower levels. The impact of the two detonating warheads tore the beast apart. Its large skull separated from its body, and was sent hurtling through the air. The mesh of teeth pierced the walls of the bridge, as if the fish intended to take one last bite before its expiration.

"Holy shit, did you see that?" Raul cried out, nudging Troy with his elbow. Troy did not answer. Everybody had seen the explosion.

"Turn this ship around, we need to search for survivors. Where are the rest of the fish?" Captain Andrews called out.

"Sir, the *Brown* has engaged the remaining fish. Their torpedoes broke the school and now their guns are taking care of the rest," the answer came.

The *Fitzgerald* turned around in the water, her deck-mounted guns firing at the breakaway groups of fish. The *Rosamilia* was gone by the time they arrived at her location, and the bodies of her crew floated on the surface, bobbing up and down in a frenzied feeding session.

"Sir, I have Captain Abbott on the line," the communications officer came across the bridge to deliver the news.

"Thank you, put him through to my ready room. You two, come with me," he said, pointing at both Raul and Troy. "Corporal Flewitt, you have the bridge while I am gone."

"Yes, sir."

Captain Abbott started talking the instant they arrived in the captain's ready room. From the tone of his voice, he was a changed man.

"Captain Abbott, how are you, how is the *Brown*?" Andrews asked, keeping his tone formal.

"We, um, we took some damage. Those things hit us from beneath, but we won," Captain Abbott answered, weeping.

"How many casualties?" Andrews asked.

"Three dead and a dozen or so injured," Captain Abbott answered. "How about you?"

"No idea on the numbers yet, sir. The big fish is gone, and the school has been broken up into small groups. We will never be able to tell if we got them all, but the main threat has been dealt with," Andrews replied, looking at Troy and Raul as he spoke. "Christopher, our job is not over yet."

"No, please tell me more," Captain Abbott asked.

For a while Captain Andrews said nothing. He studied the faces of both Troy and Raul. Taking a deep breath, he answered. Both men kept the discussion brief and to the point. Raul did most of the talking, explaining what had happened, where the beasts came from.

"Then what would you recommend?" Captain Abbott asked once Raul finished his explanation.

"I don't know. I mean, I don't even know if there is anything else down there, but, well … if I had the choice, I would say you should look to plug the gap, just in case something else, something bigger, decides to rise."

"Captain Andrews, set the course, we will follow."

CHAPTER 22

The resort island sat on the horizon, the sun rising behind it, turning what had once been a paradise into a black shroud, a tumour bulging from the ocean.

On the deck of the *Fitzgerald,* Raul and Troy stood watching the sun rise. "Do you really think it will work?" Troy asked.

"I have no idea. They put me on the spot and it just popped into my head," Raul laughed.

"Kind of like the Stay Puft Marshmallow man," Troy joked.

"Exactly."

"What are you talking about?" a voice asked.

The two men turned, and Troy smiled.

"Raul came up with a master plan to close that gash in the sea bed," Troy answered Melissa.

"Really, what are you going to have them do?" she asked.

"They are going to sink the resort island, and use it to plug the gap." Raul smiled sheepishly.

"Wow, and you convinced them that would work." Melissa looked as shocked as she sounded.

"Apparently, they were desperate," Raul laughed. "I'm just going to speak to the captain about something."

"He's not very subtle is he," Melissa said, as they watched Raul hurry away.

"Nope." Troy felt awkward. He had lost his temper in front of Melissa. He had let his anger get the better of him, and all of his self-control ran away quicker than an ice-cream truck in the middle of summer.

"How is —?"

"I'm sorry about Aiden," both spoke at once.

They laughed, nervous at first, but soon they were in each other's arms. Their embrace short, but sweet. They took comfort from their closeness, the feel of their bodies against one another. They had survived the worst that life could throw their way. All that remained was to clean up the mess and start fresh.

"I should apologize to him," Troy said after a time.

"He started it. Aiden was never the most sharing man in the world. His jealousy drove us apart years ago. This job took him away for so long every time, and I made friends… close friends and he could not accept it." Melissa took a step back. Not because she wanted the distance, but because she wanted to make sure Troy understood her seriousness. Troy was so much taller than her, she needed the room to move so as not to crane her neck.

"Maybe so, but he has been through a lot recently. I should not have attacked him like that," Troy persisted. He did not want any lingering animosity between them.

Melissa smiled and walked back into Troy's arms. They stood watching the sunrise, casting more light over the resort.

"Do you really think Raul's plan will work? I mean, sinking the island is kind of crazy," Melissa said, resting her head against Troy, just as the ship rumbled.

"I guess we are about to find out," he said as two white streaks sped through the water towards the resort.

Two more joined them, fired from the *Brown*. The pair watched as the island disappeared behind a cloud of water vapour, as the stations supporting it were blown apart. When the view cleared, the island was already sinking beneath the waves.

THE END

CHECK OUT OTHER GREAT
DEEP SEA THRILLERS

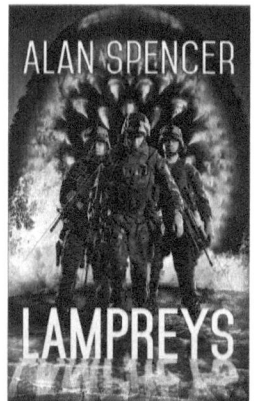

LAMPREYS
by Alan Spencer

A secret government tactical team is sent to perform a clean sweep of a private research installation. Horrible atrocities lurk within the abandoned corridors. Mutated sea creatures with insane killing abilities are waiting to suck the blood and meat from their prey.

Unemployed college professor Conrad Garfield is forced to assist and is soon separated from the team. Alone and afraid, Conrad must use his wits to battle mutated lampreys, infected scientists and go head-to-head with the biggest monstrosity of all.

Can Conrad survive, or will the deadly monsters suck the very life from his body?

DEEP DEVOTION
by M.C. Norris

Rising from the depths, a mind-bending monster unleashes a wave of terror across the American heartland. Kate Browning, a Kansas City EMT confronts her paralyzing fear of water when she traces the source of a deadly parasitic affliction to the Gulf of Mexico. Cooperating with a marine biologist, she travels to Florida in an effort to save the life of one very special patient, but the source of the epidemic happens to be the nest of a terrifying monster, one that last rose from the depths to annihilate the lost continent of Atlantis.

Leviathan, destroyer, devoted lifemate and parent, the abomination is not going to take the extermination of its brood well.

CHECK OUT OTHER GREAT
DEEP SEA THRILLERS

PREDATOR X
by C.J Waller

When deep level oil fracking uncovers a vast subterranean sea, a crack team of cavers and scientists are sent down to investigate. Upon their arrival, they disappear without a trace. A second team, including sedimentologist Dr Megan Stoker, are ordered to seek out Alpha Team and report back their findings. But Alpha team are nowhere to be found – instead, they are faced with something unexpected in the depths. Something ancient. Something huge. Something dangerous. Predator X

DEAD BAIT
by Tim Curran

A husband hell-bent on revenge hunts a Wereshark...A Russian mail order bride with a fishy secret...Crabs with a collective consciousness...A vampire who transforms into a Candiru...Zombie piranha...Bait that will have you crawling out of your skin and more. Drawing on horror, humor with a helping of dark fantasy and a touch of deviance, these 19 contemporary stories pay homage to the monsters that lurk in the murky waters of our imaginations. If you thought it was safe to go back in the water...Think Again!

CHECK OUT OTHER GREAT DEEP SEA THRILLERS

LAMPREYS
by Alan Spencer

A secret government tactical team is sent to perform a clean sweep of a private research installation. Horrible atrocities lurk within the abandoned corridors. Mutated sea creatures with insane killing abilities are waiting to suck the blood and meat from their prey.

Unemployed college professor Conrad Garfield is forced to assist and is soon separated from the team. Alone and afraid, Conrad must use his wits to battle mutated lampreys, infected scientists and go head-to-head with the biggest monstrosity of all.

Can Conrad survive, or will the deadly monsters suck the very life from his body?

DEEP DEVOTION
by M.C. Norris

Rising from the depths, a mind-bending monster unleashes a wave of terror across the American heartland. Kate Browning, a Kansas City EMT confronts her paralyzing fear of water when she traces the source of a deadly parasitic affliction to the Gulf of Mexico. Cooperating with a marine biologist, she travels to Florida in an effort to save the life of one very special patient, but the source of the epidemic happens to be the nest of a terrifying monster, one that last rose from the depths to annihilate the lost continent of Atlantis.

Leviathan, destroyer, devoted lifemate and parent, the abomination is not going to take the extermination of its brood well.

CHECK OUT OTHER GREAT
DEEP SEA THRILLERS

THEY RISE
by Hunter Shea

Some call them ghost sharks, the oldest and strangest looking creatures in the sea.

Marine biologist Brad Whitley has studied chimaera fish all his life. He thought he knew everything about them. He was wrong. Warming ocean temperatures free legions of prehistoric chimaera fish from their methane ice suspended animation. Now, in a corner of the Bermuda Triangle, the ocean waters run red. The 400 million year old massive killing machines know no mercy, destroying everything in their path. It will take Whitley, his climatologist ex-wife and the entire US Navy to stop them in the bloodiest battle ever seen on the high seas.

SERPENTINE
by Barry Napier

Clarkton Lake is a picturesque vacation spot located in rural Virginia, great for fishing, skiing, and wasting summer days away.

But this summer, something is different. When butchered bodies are discovered in the water and along the muddy banks of Clarkton Lake, what starts out as a typical summer on the lake quickly turns into a nightmare.

This summer, something new lives in the lake...something that was born in the darkest depths of the ocean and accidentally brought to these typically peaceful waters.

It's getting bigger, it's getting smarter...and it's always hungry.